SUSPECT

SUSPECT

kristin
wolden
nitz

PEACHTREE
ATLANTA

Published by
PEACHTREE PUBLISHERS
1700 Chattahoochee Avenue
Atlanta, Georgia 30318-2112
www.peachtree-online.com

Cover design by Maureen Withee
Book design and composition by Melanie McMahon Ives
Manufactured in the United States of America
10 9 8 7 6 5 4 3 2 1
First Edition

Library of Congress Cataloging-in-Publication Data
Nitz, Kristin Wolden.
  Suspect / by Kristin Wolden Nitz.
       p. cm.
  Summary: As the family gathers at her grandmother's bed-and-breakfast
for a murder mystery weekend, seventeen-year-old Jen confronts her
ambivalent feelings about her mother, who disappeared fourteen years
earlier, and about the possibility that she might be dead.
  ISBN 978-1-56145-543-0 / 1-56145-543-1
  [1. Mystery and detective stories. 2. Grandmothers--Fiction. 3. Family life--
Missouri--St. Louis--Fiction. 4. Bed and breakfast accommodations--Fiction.
5. Mothers--Fiction. 6. St. Louis (Mo.)--Fiction.] I. Title.
  PZ7.N6433St 2010
  [Fic]--dc22
                              2009040524

For Lisa Mathews,
my evil-minded editor,
and for Jeanie Ransom,
who knew how this story had to end.

With special thanks to Gretchen, who knows how
and where to use the pink and blue stuff,
as well as to Sara and Calvin, who brought my knowledge
of high school sports into the twenty-first century.

CHAPTER 1

Really, Jen, is it too much to ask?"

I pressed my lips together. I hated that question. Dad only used it when my answering "yes" would make me look selfish, inconsiderate, and completely unreasonable.

He speared a piece of Szechuan chicken with his fork and popped it into his mouth, undoubtedly hoping I'd agree to six weeks of hard labor at my grandmother's bed-and-breakfast before he finished chewing.

Was it too much to ask? No. At least it shouldn't have been. But a familiar, anxious feeling was forming under my ribs at the thought of staying out at the Schoenhaus for more than a few days. I studied the white Chinese take-out cartons sitting on our kitchen table for a few seconds, wondering why he was trying so hard to guilt me into this. Then I found the hole in his logic.

"Grandma Kay didn't ask me to help her," I pointed out. "She was just giving me first shot at the job if I wanted it. That's a big difference. I'd rather stay here in St. Louis this summer. I put in three applications today, and two of the places are hiring."

"But Jen, the summer tourist season has already started," Dad pointed out. "Training someone takes time. Your grandmother thinks making beds is an art form."

"True," I said. Then I frowned. "But wasn't she already training someone else?"

"Well, yes. But Bri only plans to put in about ten hours a week."

"Bri?" I asked. "Working? You're kidding."

Dad shrugged. "Her mom thought it would be good for her."

"Right," I said. My father had just given me another good reason to stay away from the Schoenhaus. Ten hours a week with Bri Harris was cruel and unusual punishment.

Dad paused a few seconds before adding, "Of course, I know Kent is leaving for college this fall...."

I kept my voice smooth and patient. "We broke up last week, Dad. I told you that."

Dad's eyebrows pulled together. "He was just here two nights ago."

"Yeah, helping me study for the pre-calc final," I said in my most matter-of-fact tone. Dad must have seen us sitting inches apart, leaning our heads over the same spiral notebook as Kent explained some of the odder behaviors of sines and cosines.

"We were friends before we started going out, and we're friends now," I added. "That's all." At least, that was all Kent felt.

Dad tilted his head. "Well, even if you're not dating that boy anymore, I know you'll probably want to drive back into the city to do things with your other friends. If you avoid rush hour, it takes less than an hour to get out to Augusta. I'll even cover all your gas. Just save your receipts."

I'd been filling up the old Volvo station wagon with babysitting money since the day I turned sixteen. Either someone had replaced my father with a clone who looked and sounded just like him, or something very strange was going on. I needed more excuses. Good ones. Fast. I dipped my egg roll in sweet-and-sour sauce and took a bite to give myself time to think.

"Coach Ericks wants me to work out with Leah this summer," I finally said. "If we get tougher and stronger under the basket, he thinks we could do well at districts. We might even make it to State."

"There's a hoop right next door," Dad argued. "And Mark is staying out in Augusta this summer with his dad. Playing one-on-one with him would keep you in shape, wouldn't it?"

Oh, yeah. Coach Ericks would probably be thrilled. Mark was at least two inches taller and twenty-five pounds heavier than I was and he never hesitated to "put a body" on me when we played basketball. It was doubtful he even thought of me as a girl. We'd been playing with and fighting over the same toys since we could crawl. Even though technically we weren't related—Mark was the grandson of Grandma Kay's second husband—we were family.

Dad leaned forward in his seat. "It won't be for

that long, Jen. Besides, if you're out at the Schoen-haus, I won't have to worry about you next week when I'm in D.C. for that conference."

I slammed my palms down on the table. My fork and plate rattled. "That's the real reason you want me out at the Schoenhaus, isn't it? You don't trust me."

"Honey, I do trust you, but—"

"And you're only going to be gone for six days. You just want to get me out of the way."

"I would never—," Dad began, and then stopped. After all, he had sent me out to the Schoenhaus when I was three so he could finish grad school. "That's not it at all. Come on, Jen. This would be a great chance for you to make some good money. You could help out your grandma, play basketball with Mark, hang out with Bri..."

I twitched. I couldn't help it. In fact, if I didn't have good reflexes, it would have been a full-fledged shudder.

"Ha!" Dad pointed at me in triumph. "Let me guess. Bri is the real reason you don't want to go out to the Schoenhaus. Listen, I know she wasn't very nice to you in preschool, but that was thirteen years ago."

Yeah. Thirteen years for Bri to work on her tech-nique. But if Dad wanted to blame this argument on Bri, that was all right with me. "Fine," I snapped. "If Grandma Kay is desperate, I can help her out. But oth-erwise, I don't want to go. Okay?" I sat back, crossed my arms, and waited for the Is-this-the-proper-way-to-speak-to-your-father? lecture.

But to my surprise, Dad only said okay in a quiet voice. He took a deep breath and held it as if there were more to come, then he exhaled loudly. "There's something I have to tell you," he said, running his fingers through his short, graying hair.

We sat in silence for a few seconds. "What?" I asked when he didn't go on.

"I've known about it for a while, but I made your grandma promise not to say a word until after finals."

"Okay," I said. "They're done."

Dad sighed. "I was going to let her tell you."

"Come on, Dad. Tell me what?" I asked, suddenly worried. I'd seen him act like this once before: the day he told me we had to give our cat Buster away because of my allergies.

"Now I don't buy into this," Dad said. "Not for a second. But your grandmother has really gone around the bend this time."

I relaxed. Dad made that big announcement at least twice a year. "So what's up?"

"She thinks your mother is really gone."

Um, yeah. Since my mother had left over fourteen years ago and never come back, that wasn't exactly a newsflash. There had to be something more. "And that means...?" I prompted.

"That your mother might be...dead."

"Dead?" I repeated. "Hey, I know she hasn't written in a few years, but..." I couldn't go on. Despite the hundreds of excuses I had invented for my mother—ranging from evil witches and fairies when I was younger to witness protection programs and alien abduction—I had never really considered this one. "Is that why Grandma Kay thinks my mother stopped sending me stuff?"

"No." Dad played with his chopsticks. "Your grandmother doesn't think your mother ever sent you anything. She thinks that your mother died the day she left."

The words hit me like an offensive charge I'd taken once from the Tank. After the 170-pound center had knocked me flat, I'd spent twenty seconds on the gym floor trying to suck air into my lungs while Coach Ericks knelt next to me and waited for me to say something. I had to say something now, too.

"Why?" I finally asked.

"My mother just knows it in her heart," Dad said. "She's never been big on facts."

"So what do you think?"

"I don't know." It was Dad's turn to stare at the white cartons between us. "Your mother and I had gone through a rough patch in our marriage, but I thought things were getting better. Of course, it could have all been an act so I wouldn't be suspicious...." Dad shook his head. "I never told you this and you were probably too young to remember, but your mother left me one other time. And she took you with her. It was only for a few days. I am glad—very glad—that she didn't take you with her this last time."

I was horrified to see tears in the corner of his eyes. Maybe that's the real reason big boys aren't supposed to cry. Big girls can't handle it. I tried to think of something else to say.

"But...you got divorced a long time ago. She would've had to sign something, right?"

Dad shook his head. "My lawyer hired a private

detective, and he couldn't find her. So she must not have wanted to be found. And if one spouse is absent for long enough, it's possible to get a divorce without a signature. Eventually, it was time for me—us—to move on." Dad shrugged. "I don't know where your grandmother gets these weird ideas."

"*NCIS?*" I suggested. "*CSI?* Remember, she has every season of *Murder, She Wrote* on DVD. And she runs those mystery weekends at the Schoenhaus."

Dad rubbed his temples with the tips of his fingers. Then he almost smiled. "Yeah, that's probably it. But it feels like there's something more this time. I'm worried about her, Jen. That's the real reason I'd like you to go out to the Schoenhaus."

I hadn't noticed anything wrong with Grandma Kay the last time I'd seen her. She'd always described herself as a "tough old bird." But maybe I'd missed something. "So...you want me to spy on her, then?" I asked.

"No, of course not," Dad said quickly. "I don't want a weekly report or anything. In fact, I'd actually prefer not to know any details. But if you're there, and you think that things...aren't right, you could call me."

"Okay," I said, resigned to my fate. "I'll do it."

"Wait," Dad said. "Maybe I didn't think things through all the way. This whole business could be really hard on you."

"No. I'll do it. I want to." And suddenly I did. I loved my grandmother and I couldn't stand to think that she had...well, gone around the bend, as Dad had put it. But I highly doubted that was true. "You talked me into it," I told him.

"Maybe I shouldn't have." Dad looked even more worried now.

I threw up my hands in exasperation. "I'm going," I said. "It'll be me and Grandma Kay against you."

A knock sounded at the back door.

I sat up straight. "That must be Leah. We've got that bonfire tonight. I'm late."

"Oh, right." Dad turned toward the door. "Come on in," he called.

The screen door to the garage opened and my best friend and next-door neighbor slipped into the back hall. "Oh, sorry, Mr. Schmidt," she said. "I thought you'd be done with dinner."

"No problem," Dad said. "It took longer than we expected tonight. Have a seat. Can we get you a soda or something? Water?"

"No thanks," she said.

As I choked down my now-soggy egg roll and a few clumps of cold rice covered with limp vegetables, Dad gave Leah a censored version of our discussion. He left out Grandma Kay's latest theory and my breakup with Kent. I was relieved. I always tell Leah everything, eventually—she's the closest thing I have to a sister—but I hadn't actually gotten around to telling her about Kent yet. When Dad wasn't looking, I carried my half-full plate to the kitchen and scraped the rest of my food into the trash can.

Leah pointed out that I shouldn't have to miss all the graduation parties coming up that weekend. Dad promptly agreed. He was sure Grandma Kay could handle things until Monday. I was glad Leah saved another, more touchy issue until I finished backing the Volvo out of the driveway before she pounced on me: "How do you think Kent will feel about you being gone?"

"I don't think it'll bother him too much," I said in the lightest voice I could manage. "We broke up."

"Oh, no. When?"

I hesitated, knowing that Leah wouldn't like my answer. "Um, Saturday."

"Saturday? Why did you wait so long to tell me?" she demanded.

"Well, you had that volleyball tournament all weekend. And then we were both swamped with finals and—"

"So? It would have taken you two seconds."

"I know," I said, keeping my eyes locked on the road. Branches waving overhead made irregular patterns of light and darkness on the asphalt. "But then you would've wanted a play-by-play of what happened, and I didn't want to start crying in the lunchroom or something."

"Oh. Got it," Leah said in a different tone. "Yeah, that would suck. Hey, wait a minute. Didn't I see Kent's car in your driveway on Monday night?"

"He was helping me study for the pre-calc final."

"So he gave you the old let's-be-friends speech, huh? I hate giving it. I hate getting it."

"Yeah," I agreed, even though Kent was my first real boyfriend and this my first breakup. "But everyone says that long-distance romances hardly ever work out, so this is probably the best thing. I'd just keep waiting around, never knowing when it was going to end."

"But he broke up with you," Leah said. "How can that be better?"

"I can handle the knowing," I said. "I just can't handle the *not* knowing."

Later that night, lying in bed, I thought about what Leah had said. *He broke up with you. How can that be better?* And that, I suddenly realized, was the real reason I was going to spend half my summer cleaning rooms at the Schoenhaus. I had to know what happened to my mother.

CHAPTER 2

I glanced in my rearview mirror as the Volvo climbed a steep section of Highway 94. A silver Mercedes was closing in fast. I looked back at the tree-lined country road ahead. A yellow and black sign warned of upcoming curves and only about a hundred yards remained in the passing zone. Despite all that, the driver swung out into the other lane.

I eased off the gas pedal so he could pass me more quickly. Then I saw a blue Cadillac rushing down the winding road to meet us.

I slammed on the brakes. My shoulder harness went taut. Tires squealed. The Mercedes slipped in front of me with inches between our bumpers. The driver of the other car laid on her horn in a long honk of outrage. The Mercedes accelerated away smoothly as if nothing had happened. I would have honked my horn, too, if my fingers hadn't been locked around the steering wheel in a death grip. My heart thumped in my chest as though I'd just finished the 800-meter run.

I decided that I'd better pull off the road for a minute or two to de-stress. Pale gravel crunched under my wheels as I made the turn into the Vinchgau Winery parking lot. Only three other cars were there. The silver Mercedes wasn't among them, but I hadn't thought it would be. If the driver had been making stop after stop at the wineries for free samples, I would probably be trapped in my car right now, waiting for someone to cut me out of a twisted hunk of metal.

I put the Volvo into park, turned off the ignition, and felt the engine shudder to a halt. Then I sat for a moment in silence before getting out of the car, still feeling jittery from the close call. I wasn't in any hurry to go in anyway. I always felt a little out of place here at the winery. One glance at me would make it clear to anyone that I was too young to drink anything but the sparkling juices. I'd always been tall, but it had never fooled people into believing that I was older than my age. Everybody who worked at the Vinchgau probably knew me by sight anyway since its owner, Barbara Martin, was Grandma Kay's best friend.

A bell jangled. I turned to see a pair of middle-aged women leaving the tasting rooms. Each of them carried a bottle wrapped in red tissue paper. I watched for a moment, wondering whether Barbara might come out. She didn't.

I left the car behind and walked across a flagstone patio to the gazebo. My knees shook a little as I sat down on a bench overlooking the floodplain. The Missouri River was a thin, silver line in the distance, but I'd seen it fill the fields below with a churning sea of muddy brown water after heavy rains. I took a few deep breaths of the warm, humid air. The tightness in my neck and shoulders began to ease.

I heard voices below me. Not the words. Just the sounds. A path led from the winery down to the Katy Trail, a bike path that ran for over two hundred miles along the old railroad right-of-way. Barbara had told me that she didn't object to having a few extra cars parked in her lot for the day. Most hikers bought a few bottles of wine before they left.

"Hey, Jen. What's up?"

I choked back a squawk of surprise as I recognized the guy grinning at me from the edge of the flagstone patio: Mark, my "uncousin." Scaring me had always been one of his favorite hobbies. He rested his forearms on the handlebars of his mountain bike, his blue eyes sparkling.

"I wasn't exactly being quiet," he said, in the deep gravelly voice that had earned him the role of the Beast in his high school's spring musical. "I thought you saw me. You look kind of funny. Is everything okay?"

"A Mercedes nearly ran me off the road a few minutes ago," I told him. "It freaked me out a little."

"Did you honk at him?" Mark swiped at his kickstand with the toe of his Nike basketball shoes.

"No, but this other car did. I still don't know how the Mercedes got back in front of me in time."

Mark's eyebrows pulled together. "Whoa. I think I might have heard the whole thing. It was up on the bluffs, right? I thought someone was going to get plowed for sure."

"Yeah," I said. "Me." For half a second, I could

practically see the silver car cutting in front of me again.

Mark dropped onto the bench beside me. Our shoulders touched briefly and then he pulled away a few inches.

"So what are you doing here?" I asked.

He shrugged. "Buying a bottle of water."

"Well, go get it," I said. His short dark hair was damp. A line of sweat trickled down the side of his face. His shirt clung to his back and shoulders, outlining a shape that Leah had described as "on the skinny side of hot."

"Aren't you going in?"

"No," I said. "I don't need Barbara telling Grandma Kay that I can't handle the roads. So how long are you stuck out here?"

"The whole summer," Mark said cheerfully. "I'll be working at a bike shop on the Katy Trail and helping Dad with the grapes."

"How does your mom feel about that?"

Mark gazed out over the vineyards. "She needs to put in a lot of hours on some big case that's going to trial in July. So the parental units managed to work out all the visitation stuff without fighting this time. Plus, I've got a car, so I can go back and forth when I want."

"Sounds like you like it out here," I said, surprised.

"I do. It's not like when we were little kids stuck playing together every day. I got to know a lot of the kids around here when I stayed with Dad during fifth grade. We get together for volleyball and stuff."

"Volleyball," I repeated. "That sounds like fun. Who plays?"

Mark reeled off a list of names. Bri wasn't on it. Good.

"And sometimes," Mark went on, "we'll head into Chesterfield for a movie. Maybe what's-his-name could come meet us if you want to go sometime."

"What's-his-name?"

"You know. That Kent guy."

"That Kent guy and I aren't going out anymore."

"Oh," Mark said. Curiosity burned behind his eyes. But if he wasn't going to ask, I wasn't going to offer an explanation.

"So what happened?"

I shrugged. "We decided to go back to being friends."

"Huh," Mark said.

"We really are friends," I insisted. "I went to his graduation open house last weekend."

Mark held his hand up in front of his face like a shield. "Hey, I believe you."

I caught sight of the time on Mark's watch. "Whoa, I'm late. I'd better get going or Grandma Kay might get worried."

"See you tonight then," Mark said. I must have looked surprised, because he hurried to explain. "Grandma Kay's having a Welcome Jen dinner before the meeting of the mystery weekend executive board."

"Uh-oh. When's the mystery this year?" I asked.

"It starts Friday."

"Guess I'll be busy then," I said. Every room in the Schoenhaus would be full, and I'd have to help get them ready. Twenty of my grandmother's friends usually came to put on a murder weekend each year. Not everyone stayed on site, as Grandma Kay's bed-and-breakfast wasn't big enough for that, and some people, like Uncle Steve and Aunt Lynn, lived nearby. But still, the place would be crazy.

"So who's planning it this year?" I asked.

"Grandma Kay," Mark answered. "She said this is going to be one mystery weekend that everyone will remember."

CHAPTER 3

The brightly painted upper stories of the Schoenhaus rose above the green lines of Uncle Steve's vineyard as I rounded the curve of the highway. One of Grandma Kay's brochures described the house as Late Empire, but to my inexpert eyes it looked like a typical Victorian—complete with cupola, tower, balconies, bay windows, enormous porches, and more trim than you could shake a paintbrush at.

The Schoenhaus had been built a few miles west of Augusta by a wealthy St. Louis family. According to family history, my Grandpa David had been talking about leaving his brokerage house for years when the house had come on the market. He always claimed that the decision to convert the old house into a bed-and-breakfast had been based on the glowing report of the housing inspector, the growing popularity of the nearby wineries, and other sound financial factors.

But Grandma Kay insisted that it was their ten-minute walk through the overgrown backyard that did it. For the chance to reclaim the garden, he was suddenly able to justify things he'd called "insur-mountable obstacles" just the day before. He happily made the switch from high finance to Schoenhaus handyman. I never had a chance to get to know Grandpa David. He died a year before I was born.

I turned right onto the long paved driveway. A wide green lawn stretched out to the left. At its far edge, hundreds of daylilies bloomed in the shadow of the woods. A metal fence draped with vines separated Grandma Kay's property from that of Uncle Steve, Mark's dad. Of course, Uncle Steve wasn't my real uncle any more than Mark was my cousin. But the son and grandson of Grandma Kay's second husband were family in every way that mattered.

A red Miata convertible was the only other car in the lot. As I pulled up next to it, I recognized Uncle Doug's license plate: BLT4SPD. Technically, he wasn't my uncle, either. He and Dad were first cousins who had grown up practically as brothers. It helped, I suppose, that they had both inherited the Schmidt family flair for understanding money. Dad wrote totally incomprehensible articles on economic theory while Uncle Doug advised private investors. But they could both talk about the money supply, interest rates, and the trade deficit for hours. I usually left the room when they got started.

I opened my car door and popped the trunk. As I pulled out my suitcases, I could smell the white climbing roses that crisscrossed the front porch's stone foundation on the right side of the front steps. To the left, a circular porch curved out. The whole scene looked like a cover photo for *Better Homes and Gardens*. Through the brightly painted railings, I could see dark rattan chairs and bright floral cushions.

My suitcases banged against my legs as I climbed the eight steps to the porch. A few strides brought me to the walnut front door. I pushed it open, stepped into the black-and-white marble entryway, and spotted Grandma Kay standing behind the antique front desk. She seemed to be sifting through a stack of papers. Her chin-length silver-gray hair framed her face, and a necklace of polished green stones swung from her neck.

"Aha!" she exclaimed as she held up an envelope. "So that's where you've been hiding."

Grandma Kay had a habit of talking to inanimate objects, so this didn't worry me at all. In fact, I began to think that Dad had overreacted about Grandma Kay. She seemed perfectly fine. Her face was lightly made up. The lipstick and eye shadow looked like they had been carefully coordinated with the jewel tones of her boatneck cotton tunic and calf-length rayon skirt. She scanned the paper for a few seconds before turning to me.

"Jen! Your father called. He was worried."

I set down my suitcases. "I'm a good driver."

"Of course you are, dear." Grandma Kay's high-heeled boots clicked on the marble as she crossed the floor to meet me. She stood on tiptoe and threw her arms around my neck. "But he heard about an accident by the Daniel Boone Bridge on the radio," she added. "Naturally, he wasn't about to call your cell phone while you were driving. Any problems on the road?"

"Just a near miss with a Mercedes," I admitted, in case Mark said anything about it later. "But otherwise everything went fine."

"Good. Thank you so much for coming, Jen. Maddie felt terribly guilty about breaking her arm until she heard you were willing to help out."

"How's she doing?" I asked.

"Much better now, thank goodness. It nearly scared me to death when I heard her tumbling down the stairs like that. She'll drop by later this week, though, so you'll get to see her."

"Good," I said.

"I'm glad you're here. We have so much to talk about," Grandma Kay said. "But now, I really must get back to Doug. He's doing my biannual financial planning review. You know, stocks, bonds, insurance, estate planning—all those things I don't understand. I don't know what I would have done all these years without him to help me with money matters. He'll be staying for dinner, of course." Grandma Kay went back behind the desk, grabbed a key, and handed it to me. "Why don't you unpack, dear? I'm giving you the room you had last Christmas."

"With the tower? Really? But you can't."

"Why not? You love that room, don't you?"

"Yes, but—"

"And you're doing me a big, big favor, aren't you? Plus, you'll get better reception on your cell phone up there than you would down in the basement with me."

That was true. "But aren't the weekends really busy? You'll need the room for guests."

"If you want to rent out your room, you can come take your usual spot downstairs. I'll split the booking with you."

"It doesn't get much fairer than that," another voice said.

Uncle Doug was standing in the hallway to the kitchen. He grinned at me over his reading glasses, his eyes crinkling at the corners. Feature for feature, Uncle Doug looked a lot like Dad—except that my father wasn't even close to what Leah would call "a hot old guy"—and Uncle Doug was.

"I would have thought you'd say that it wasn't a sound financial decision," Grandma Kay said.

"Keeping your employees happy is always a sound financial decision," Uncle Doug said in a mock-serious tone. "Right, Jen?"

"Right," I said.

"I'm sorry I took so long, Doug. I just found my goals-for-the-year notes." Grandma Kay handed him the phone company envelope that was covered with her small, almost illegible handwriting. "I meant to copy it over onto something else, but..."

"That's all right. The little break gave me some time to put my papers back in order." Uncle Doug turned to me. "She kept leaping around from page to page. My nice orderly financial overview is in a shambles, so I don't know what I've covered and what I haven't. You wouldn't think that rampant disorganization could be catching."

"Disorganization?" Grandma Kay protested. "I'm not disorganized."

Uncle Doug said nothing. He glanced over the counter at the stacks of paper scattered around the reception desk.

"I know exactly where everything is," Grandma Kay insisted. Uncle Doug looked pointedly at the envelope she had been waving for emphasis. "Well, most of the time," she said. "If I am so difficult, why haven't you handed my account over to one of your lowly assistants?"

"I could never be that cruel to them," Uncle Doug joked. Then he said more seriously, "No, Aunt Kay. I wouldn't want to lose my oldest client."

"Oldest?" Grandma Kay echoed in mock outrage.

I smiled. Grandma Kay and Uncle Doug could go back and forth like this for hours.

Uncle Doug studied the list. "Number one: walk more. Good idea, but there's not much I can do about that. Number two: shut down for an extra week during January. Well, you certainly deserve a break, Aunt Kay. And you can more than afford it. Most of your Valentine's weekend bookings should be made already. Number three: shift more assets into the bond market. That's not a bad idea. I have several buying opportunities in mind. Number four: find out who..." Uncle Doug paused, squinted, and lowered the piece of paper to arm's length. "Find out who murdered Ellen?"

Ellen. My mother. I took a deep breath.

Grandma Kay snatched the piece of paper out of his hand. "I didn't write that down, did I?"

"I'm afraid so," Uncle Doug said.

I twitched. For just a second, he had sounded exactly like Dad.

"You weren't supposed to see that," Grandma Kay said, as if Uncle Doug had just discovered his Christmas present on a shelf in the hallway closet.

"What's going on? Is this about your mystery weekend?" Uncle Doug's frown deepened.

Grandma Kay tilted her head. "In a way. Let's move on to number five."

Uncle Doug glanced at me. My face must have told him something because he didn't let the subject go. "You don't mean Jen's mother, do you? Has there been...news?"

"Well, nooooooo..." Grandma Kay pressed her lips together for a moment. "I suppose I would have talked to you about this at some point. Frankly, I don't think Ellen ever made it to New York. I think my poor daughter-in-law was murdered right here."

"What?" Uncle Doug asked. His horrified eyes flicked back to mine. I realized that I was still holding my breath. I let it out in an uneasy whoosh and lowered myself slowly into one of the chairs by the front desk.

"Well, not right *here*," Grandma Kay said. "I mean she never left Missouri. Someone just made it look as if she did. Ellen would never have just disappeared forever like that. Especially without making sure she had a legal right to see Jen." Grandma Kay turned to me. "Your mother adored you, dear. She had so many big plans for all of the things that you were going to do together. If she were alive, she would have fought to spend time with you. I just know it. I can feel it in my gut."

Maybe Grandma Kay was trying to make me feel better, but her words were like a knife to the heart. I squeezed my eyes shut against the memories of all those Mother's Days without a mother—all those basketball parents' nights when most of the other girls walked across the gym with two parents, even if they were divorced.

"Jen, are you okay?" Uncle Doug asked.

"Yeah," I lied, opening my eyes. "This is all pretty weird to think about."

"Of course it is," Uncle Doug said. He glared at Grandma Kay. "I hope you have some facts to back up your little theory. Because otherwise you'll put Jen and Jerry through hell all over again, and that's not fair to them."

Grandma Kay crossed her arms defiantly. "I'm well aware of that, Doug. But how are we supposed to get at the truth unless we talk about it? What if we've been looking at everything the wrong way all this time? Is that fair to Ellen?" She held up a hand. "Never mind. Don't answer that. We have to finish our review before everyone shows up for dinner. Go get settled in, please, Jen." Without another word, she lifted her chin and strode toward the kitchen.

"We'll talk later," Uncle Doug whispered to me before trotting after Grandma Kay.

Since there was nothing else I could do for the moment, I got up and lugged my suitcases over to the main staircase. Once I reached the first landing under the Tiffany stained-glass window, I stopped to get a better grip—on everything.

If my mother had really died back when I was

three, then who had sent me all those cards, letters, and presents from New York? The gifts always seemed to be exactly what I wanted, which was usually what the other girls in school had, and—most importantly—what Dad refused to buy me. I could never write her a thank-you note. None of the letters had a return address. The packages did, but only the address of the store or mail order catalog that had shipped the gift. Then, years ago, the cards and presents had stopped. It had taken me a while, but I'd gotten over that. Mostly. But now that half-anxious, half-hopeful feeling near the bottom of my ribcage was creeping back. Maybe I could make it go away if I blasted some tunes on my iPod. But I didn't feel like digging through my stuff on the landing to find it. I kept climbing.

The third-floor hallway featured watercolor paintings by Aunt Lynn. Mark's stepmom said it was like having her own private gallery, except she didn't have to worry about staffing it. I stopped to check out the newest painting, a view of the Schoenhaus gardens in early spring. Crocuses and daffodils bloomed in the rock garden.

I reached my room, unlocked the door, and pushed it open. Rose wallpaper and an antique canopy bed decorated my favorite room in the Schoenhaus. A wide, comfortable chair and massive ottoman filled most of the small, circular tower room. It was the perfect place to read. But a new decoration sat on the bedside table next to the alarm clock. Instead of an antique knickknack or an Aunt Lynn original, it was a framed photograph of Kent and me. Grandma Kay had taken it in front of the limo on prom night. I set my suitcases just inside the door and strode across the room to pick it up.

Grandma Kay had asked for an action shot. Kent had spun me around a few times and then bent me back in a classic ballroom dip. At the moment the shutter had clicked, I was laughing up at Kent with surprised delight. He was gazing at me with an expression of—what? Not love. He'd made that very clear nine days ago, in the kindest way possible. He was headed off to the University of Chicago in a few months and he'd said I should be free to enjoy my senior year of high school.

But prom had been a magical night, from the second he'd shown up on my doorstep in a great-fitting black tux. The blue of his vest and bow tie brought out his eyes and worked beautifully with my dress. That dress. I studied the gold, blue, and purple beadwork on the shoulder straps and along the low V-neck. The pattern printed onto the pale turquoise background started with deep purple flowers that shifted gradually to black. The thin, wavy, metallic gold lines that ran through the fabric—Kent called them low-amplitude, low frequency sine waves, or something like that—didn't show up in the photograph.

I'd felt like a princess that night, and Kent had treated me like one: a limo for the night, reservations at the revolving restaurant overlooking the Arch, a series of spins and dips on the dance floor.

I sighed and set the photo back down in its place. I would have to tell Grandma Kay that I appreciated her gift, even though Kent and I weren't going out anymore. I'd only been at the Schoenhaus ten minutes and Grandma Kay had managed to bring up both my mother's disappearance and my break-up with Kent.

This was turning into one tough afternoon.

CHAPTER 4

When I called my dad, he picked up midway through the first ring. "Hello?"

"I made it," I said. "So you can stop worrying now."

"Glad to hear it," Dad replied, ignoring my tone. He proceeded to go over his schedule in great detail and then started reading out a list of numbers where I could leave messages while he was in meetings.

"Dad," I said in exasperation. "I can text you or leave a message. You can call me back. Everything's going to be fine."

"Famous last words?"

"Dad," I said through clenched teeth.

"Sorry. How's Grandma Kay?"

"She's fine. Really."

"All right. I love you, sweetheart," he said.

"I love you, too, Dad."

When I finally got him to hang up, the odd, worried feeling in the depths of my stomach had gotten worse. I felt like running up and down the stairs a few times to get rid of all my nervous energy. Instead, I found my iPod and put on my favorite basketball pregame playlist while I unpacked.

When I finished, I shoved my empty suitcases into the closet. Except for a few wrinkles on the bedspread, the room looked much as it had when I'd come in. But this was the Schoenhaus. Even my room needed to look perfect. I twitched the covers until they lay straight. Then I picked up the key from the dresser, put it in my pocket, and went downstairs to see if Grandma Kay needed any help with dinner.

The smell of garlic, sausage, oregano, and tomato sauce greeted me on the landing. Lasagna?

I opened the door to the kitchen, the one room in the Schoenhaus that didn't look like it belonged in a magazine. The commercial stainless-steel dishwasher, the coffeemaker, and the rack of six-foot-wide ovens were meant for a restaurant, not a private home. A standard-sized stove sat in one corner. It beeped at me in a demanding sort of way.

I cracked open the oven door. Inside, the sauce bubbled and the mozzarella cheese had turned a golden brown. The oven beeped again. Done. Since it was already 6:20, I pulled the two pans out and replaced them with two loaves of French bread that had already been wrapped in aluminum foil. Then I started washing the pots that had been left in the sink to soak.

A buzzer announced that the front door had opened and the sharp click of high heels echoed across the floors. A moment later, Grandma Kay's friend Barbara swept into the room holding a wine bottle by the neck.

"Jen, hello. Where's your grandmother?"

"Downstairs with Uncle Doug, discussing money stuff. She should be here soon."

Barbara reached into a drawer and pulled out a stainless steel corkscrew. As she peeled the foil off the top of the bottle, she said, "You know, Jen, the next time you stop by the Vinchgau, you could actually come inside and say hello."

"I'm sorry—," I began, but Barbara cut me off.

"No need to apologize. Mark explained about the idiot in the Mercedes and how you had to hurry in case your grandmother was worried. She's had a lot on her mind with the mystery weekend and so on." Barbara's voice dropped. "I hear your dad told you about Kay's latest theory."

"So you know about it, too?"

Barbara nodded. "Of course. Your grandma and I talked it all out. I'm glad she listened to me for once. But don't worry, the only people who know about this whole idea are you, me, and your father."

"And Uncle Doug."

Barbara frowned. "How did he find out?"

Grandma Kay flung open the door leading from the basement and hurtled into the room. She stopped when she saw the two pans of lasagna sitting side by side.

"Oh, thank goodness!"

"No. Thank Jen," Barbara drawled.

"Thank you, Jen," Grandma Kay said promptly. "You saved the lasagna from turning into leather. These things with Doug always take longer than we expect. And he was a bit distracted today, the poor dear."

"Why did you have to tell him about the Ellen thing?" Barbara demanded. "There's no point in getting everyone all upset—not until we come up with some kind of realistic plan."

"Well, I didn't mean to—," Grandma Kay began, but stopped when the back door swung open.

Aunt Lynn entered first, carrying a glass bowl of lettuce. Mark followed his stepmom with a plate of white chocolate and cranberry cookies. Uncle Steve came in last and closed the door.

Aunt Lynn smiled up at me from her height of five feet. "Good to see you, Jen. How was finals week?"

"Long," I said.

"Funny, Mark said the same thing," Uncle Steve observed.

My uncousin rolled his eyes. He'd showered since I'd seen him last. His dark hair was still wet. I caught the faintest scent of his shampoo as he joined me at the counter.

"Your timing is perfect," Grandma Kay said. "Doug will join us as soon as he finishes trying to fit all of his papers back into his briefcase. I just need a bit of help with a few last-minute things...."

Within seconds, we all had our assignments. Uncle Steve cut the lasagna into squares, Aunt Lynn tossed her salad, Mark grated Parmesan cheese, and I arranged the bread on two plates. Barbara disappeared to pour the wine. When Uncle Doug thumped up the stairs from the basement, Grandma Kay handed him a relish tray and we all trooped into the sunroom.

Years ago, Grandma Kay had hired an architect to design a Victorian conservatory for the back of the

Schoenhaus to serve as a dining area. Somehow he'd managed to make the slanting glass and metal roof look like it had grown out of the back of the house. One of the tables was set for dinner; the rest were laid out with cups, saucers, and bowls for the traditional breakfasts.

I grabbed a spot across from Mark because I knew how the conversations would go. Grandma Kay, Barbara, and Aunt Lynn wouldn't be able to stop themselves from discussing the tourist trade, even if they tried. Uncle Doug and Uncle Steve were both hardcore St. Louis Cardinals fans, so I knew they'd want to dissect the last series against the Cubs. I got Mark started on final exam horror stories so he wouldn't get sucked into the baseball conversation. I needed someone to talk to.

Just as we finished dessert, an electronic ring cut through the air. Grandma Kay pulled her phone out of her pocket and studied the screen. "Goodness. I lost track of the time. Ally Harris will be here at any minute for the mystery board meeting."

Ally Harris was Bri's mom. It still baffled me how the nastiest girl I knew had one of the nicest moms I'd ever met.

"So what's the mystery going to be about this year?" Mark asked.

"It's supposed to be set in a mansion along the Hudson River," Grandma Kay said. "An elderly eccentric—that would be me—is holding a house party in honor of her niece, who is dropping out of the family law firm after writing a best-selling semiautobiographical novel. Some of the guests are very annoyed at how versions of themselves were portrayed in the book. Lynn has the artistic temperament, so she's taking on the part of the novelist. Steve will most conveniently play the part of her sulky husband."

Uncle Steve grinned.

"Barbara will portray Lynn's old writing mentor, who never had anything published outside of small literary magazines," Grandma Kay continued. "This dysfunctional bunch should make for a lot of fun."

"I think I've identified your victim already," Uncle Doug said.

"So soon?" Grandma Kay asked, sounding disappointed. "Because I think it will be a challenge for the club. Only the planner, villain, and victim know for sure who the victim will be. And you never know what's going to happen—a robbery, a murder, a disappearance. Plus, if anyone gets too close to the truth, we may have a second crime of opportunity. It'll be a very interesting weekend."

Uncle Doug leaned back in his chair. "But this is really about Ellen, isn't it? You as much as said so earlier today."

"Ellen?" Uncle Steve blinked. "Ellen who?"

"Jen's mother," Uncle Doug said in a flat voice. "Jerry's ex-wife."

"Oh," Uncle Steve said, but he looked even more confused.

"What? Have you found out something new about Ellen? Did something happen to her?" Aunt Lynn asked, her eyes wide with horror. She looked from me to Grandma Kay.

My grandmother threw up her hands. "How many

times do I have to go through this today?" she asked
the ceiling fan. I wondered the exact same thing.

"One more time, it seems," Barbara said, "since it's
out on the table now."

"So you knew about this?" Uncle Doug demanded.

Barbara shrugged. "When Kay told me about her
original mystery plot, I saw some parallels. I helped
her change the story enough so that no one outside
the family would have a clue."

"You did a very good job," Aunt Lynn said. Her
eyes were bright and her voice was unsteady. "But you
still haven't said what happened to Ellen."

Grandma Kay rested her fingertips on the green
linen tablecloth. "Well, here it is. I don't believe she
abandoned my son and granddaughter fourteen years
ago. I think she was taken from them."

I saw Mark's whole body stiffen. His brain must
have instantly translated "taken" to "murdered."

In the long silence that followed, I suddenly
became aware of the soft hum of the fans overhead.

"But Jen used to get presents from Ellen for Christmas," Uncle Doug finally said.

"Sent by the murderer," Grandma Kay announced,
"so no one would go looking for the truth."

"But weren't there letters, too?" Aunt Lynn asked,
looking at me.

"Faked." Grandma Kay slapped the table for
emphasis. "Cleverly faked."

"Uh, yeah, there were letters," I said. "But I
haven't gotten any for a long time."

"What did they say?" Uncle Steve asked.

"Stuff," I answered. I didn't dare say anything else

or my voice might start to shake. I knew what every letter said, though. At one time I'd almost had them memorized.

"Did you keep any of them?" Barbara asked.

"Um, I think so." Of course I did.

"Really?" Grandma Kay's voice rose in delight. "I was hoping you might have."

I shrugged. "They're probably still buried somewhere in my closet."

"Oh, wonderful!" Grandma Kay straightened. "Then we may have actual physical evidence. Fingerprints. Postmarks. Maybe even DNA. We'll go through it all with gloves right away. Every scrap."

I looked down at Grandma Kay's hands as they gripped the table's edge. They reminded me of a harpy's claws, ready to tear and shred. Worse, there was a burning look in her eyes that reminded me of people in movies right before they were about to snap. If that's what Dad had seen, I knew now why he was worried.

"Aunt Kay," Uncle Doug said, "surely you're not suggesting that Jen drive home right this instant and collect them?"

Grandma Kay blinked rapidly. Her fingers relaxed their grip. "Of course not. We've waited this long. We can wait a bit longer. There are too many things to do between today and Friday afternoon. The show must go on." She paused for an instant. "You should join us, Doug. I've had a cancellation. Bill Benton had emergency gall bladder surgery. He'll be fine, but it leaves a big hole in my plot since he's one of the senior partners in the law firm."

"Sorry, Aunt Kay. It's not my idea of a fun weekend," Uncle Doug said.

"Steve didn't think he'd like them either, and now he's on the executive board," Grandma Kay said. "And, if you insist, I'll even charge you full price for your room."

"Oh, no." Uncle Doug shook his head. "I wouldn't want you to make an exception in my case."

"Then you'll come?"

"I suppose."

The tension in the room eased at the familiar scene of Grandma Kay talking someone into something that they didn't want to do.

"That's settled, then," Grandma Kay said brightly. "The mystery begins at six. That's when everyone will officially get into character and start dropping clues. Dinner is at seven. I'll e-mail you your character sketch and responsibilities later this evening."

Uncle Doug pushed his chair back from the table. "I'd better leave now if I'm going to spend the weekend out here. I have some things I need to take care of."

Grandma Kay smiled. "Poor boy. You work too hard. We'll see you Friday, then. You can arrive as early as three o'clock for check-in."

"All right," Uncle Doug said. "I suppose I can suffer through this mystery weekend thing once. Jen, will you come with me? I have something for you in the car."

"Sure." I pulled my napkin from my lap and got to my feet.

I followed Uncle Doug out of the sunroom and

down the polished wood hall in silence. After we crossed the front porch and made it partway down the steep front steps, Uncle Doug asked, "Have you known about this crazy idea of Kay's for a while, Jen? You didn't seem surprised."

"Dad told me about it after finals."

"So he knows about all of this, too?"

"Yeah. Everything except the mystery weekend."

Uncle Doug turned around to stare back up at the porch of the Schoenhaus. The long shadows of the setting midsummer sun magnified the wrinkles around his eyes. I noticed more strands of gray in his hair. Finally, he said, "I'm betting Jerry sent you here to keep an eye on things, didn't he?"

"I'm afraid so," I said.

"Well, maybe that's a good thing. Sometimes the past can become more real for us older folk than the present." Uncle Doug sighed. "Both your dad and I have been worrying that the Schoenhaus is too much for your grandma now. She doesn't need the money. In fact, she never did. In some ways, it's been a big, profitable dollhouse. Maddie has taken on more of the load over the years, but I don't know if it's enough."

"Grandma Kay is tough," I said. "I can't even keep up with her some days. She can clean me under the rug."

"I suppose. But before I forget..." Uncle Doug walked over to his red convertible, opened the driver's side door, and reached behind the seat. He pulled out a package the size of a softball. It was wrapped in green paper crisscrossed with curling silver ribbons. He handed the box to me with a nod.

"You really did have something for me," I said.

"An extremely late birthday present. Go ahead. Open it."

The box was surprisingly heavy for its size. Uncle Doug held out his hands to take the wrapping paper after I peeled it off. I opened the lid and pulled out a wad of tissue paper. A green metal frog crouched in the bottom of the box.

"Oh, I remember this guy," I said in delight. "I couldn't afford him because I'd spent all my money on Christmas presents."

Uncle Doug shoved his hands into his pockets and grinned at me. "I could tell how much you liked it. I'd already bought you something for Christmas, but the frog is more of a summer gift anyway. I'd say that he belongs in your backyard."

"No way. He's staying on my dresser so no one can take him. Thanks, Uncle Doug."

"You're welcome."

"So," I said. "I guess I'll see you this weekend."

"Yes, but I'm not looking forward to it," Uncle Doug grumbled. "I don't understand what's so fun about sitting around and waiting for one of your fellow characters to drop dead."

"Hey, I did a body count once during one of those old Arnold Schwarzenegger movies that you and Dad like so much," I said. "I think I lost track around sixty."

"You've got me there," Uncle Doug said, chuckling. "But that reminds me of one more thing. Lisa sent something along for you, too." He reached under the driver's seat and pulled out a paperback book.

"Thanks," I said as he handed it to me. I glanced at the crocodile on the cover. This must be one of the mysteries Uncle Doug's latest girlfriend had told me about. We'd talked about books for almost half an hour during a backyard barbecue Dad had thrown to celebrate the end of St. Louis University's spring term. "You know," I said, "I bet Lisa would love the whole murder weekend thing. Maybe you should bring her along. I'm sure Grandma Kay could work her into the plot."

"A whole weekend at the Schoenhaus? I don't think so. It might frighten her away forever. I'm not taking any chances until—" Uncle Doug stopped and pressed his lips together.

"You're getting married?" I shrieked with delight.

"Nothing is settled. So you can keep that to yourself," Uncle Doug ordered, but he couldn't keep from smiling.

"I won't tell anyone," I said. "Not even Grandma Kay."

"Especially not Kay," Uncle Doug said. "So, when's your dad leaving for his conference?"

"Tomorrow morning."

"Well, call me if you need anything then, okay?"

"I will," I said. "But everything will be fine."

"I hope so." Uncle Doug climbed into his Miata and looked up at me. "You take care. Try not to let any of this get to you."

I nodded. I could try.

As Uncle Doug drove away I studied the back cover of the book. Tombs and mummies in 1880s Egypt? It looked like a good escape, and I needed one.

A dark blue car pulled into the driveway right after Uncle Doug pulled out. Its chrome-plated grill and sleek styling made it look old, expensive, and oddly familiar. I suddenly recognized the Jaguar. Bri's mom must be here for the meeting. I waited to say hello. I'd always liked Mrs. Harris.

The car door on the driver's side swung open. "Hi, Jen!" Mrs. Harris called as she stepped out. "It's so good to see you. When I told Bri you were going to be here tonight, she wanted to come, too. And I had to agree it would be such a nice chance for you girls to catch up before you start working together."

Catch up with what? We'd never been friends. Yeah, we'd been stuck with each other on a few occasions, but I'd hardly seen Bri since she was old enough to babysit herself. The passenger door opened an instant later. Bri emerged with her cell phone in her hand. She slid it into her purse before rushing toward me with outstretched arms like we were a couple of cheerleaders who hadn't seen each other since lunch.

"Jen!" she called. "Hi! How are you?"

"Hi!" I said, raising my voice a half octave to match her tone. "I'm good. How about you?"

"Great!" she said, her voice rising even higher. As she got closer, it was clear that she was really planning to hug me.

This did not mean that we were suddenly buddies. The girl was a total fake, especially in front of adults. As I leaned down for the hug, I felt like a moose. I'm not fat or anything. In fact, Coach Ericks had hinted that I'd be able to block out under the basket better if I put on a few pounds of muscle this summer. But Bri was six inches shorter than me with the build of a ballet dancer.

She stepped back. Up close, her white-blonde hair looked like something off the cover of *Teen Vogue*. Her makeup was more subtle, but just as perfect.

"Wow, Jen," she said. "Summer has just started, and you're so tan already."

"Track practice," I said.

"Oh." Bri nodded. "Guess that explains your feet, then."

I barely stopped myself from looking down at my flip-flops. I knew that the tops of my feet were pale beyond belief. All the girls on the team hated track tan.

"Uh, yeah," I said.

The front door to the Schoenhaus swung open, and my uncousin stepped out onto the porch.

"Mark!" Bri squealed. She pounded up the steps two at a time and flung herself at him. His arms closed around her as he lifted her off the ground.

I had a very bad feeling about this.

CHAPTER 5

No, I thought. Not Bri and Mark. It couldn't be. I remembered how Mark had fallen for Bri back in fifth grade. He was the new kid, and she'd already worked her way through all the other boys in the small Augusta elementary school. Poor Mark had a crush on her for at least a year. But I was pretty sure that he had a girlfriend back home these days. One thing was obvious, though. Bri hadn't come to see me; she'd come to see Mark. I slowly climbed the porch steps. Mrs. Harris followed.

Mark grinned at Bri as he set her down. "Hey, Bri, what's up?"

"Nothing much," she said. "I haven't seen you in forever."

"Yes, you have," Mark said. "You came to the closing night of the play, remember?"

"Right. You were sooooo good." Bri lightly touched his arm. "Our drama club has been trying to talk our director into doing *Beauty and the Beast* for years now."

"Well, it's kind of expensive to put on with all the

sets and costume rentals," Mark said. "But we wound up coming out ahead on ticket sales. I swear, every little girl and her mom from twenty miles around came to see it. Right, Jen?" He turned to me.

I made myself smile. "Um, right," I said.

"I'll have to tell our director," Bri said.

"You need a lot of baritones for the lead parts," Mark told her. "So if you're stuck with nothing but tenors, you can forget it."

"Oh, I'd love to play Belle," Bri said. "That's who I was on the Disney Princess Facebook quiz."

"You're kidding," I said before I could stop myself.

"No surprise there," Mrs. Harris put in. "I think we wore out the videotape when she was little."

"Mmm," I said. Belle's first song in *Beauty and the Beast* was about how much she looked down on everyone in her poor provincial town. Maybe Bri would be perfect for the part.

"I'll bet you know the words to all the songs, too," Bri said with a warm smile at me.

"Oh, sure," I agreed. After all, saying no would have been rude in three or four different ways.

"Well, you kids have fun," Mrs. Harris said. "I'd better get inside."

"Everyone was still in the sunroom a minute ago," Mark said.

"Thanks," Mrs. Harris said. "See you all later."

Bri's fingers closed around Mark's wrist. She pulled him toward one of the loveseats on the circular porch to the left of the front door. I dropped into a nearby chair. Bri bombarded my uncousin with questions about the auditions. How did his director pair up the readers? Which scenes and songs were chosen? Did they do things differently in the callbacks?

After Bri finished her interrogation, she and Mark started trading stories about their various shows. I half-listened. My only acting stories were about basketball. Leah's dad had given me advice about grunting authentically during a foul. "Stop holding it in when someone clobbers you," he'd said. "Let the ref know there was contact."

I barely kept myself from snorting when Mark started telling Bri about the best products for removing certain types of stage makeup. Apparently the gunk Mark had worn when he played Banquo during the ghost scenes in *Macbeth* was the worst. That play is all about death, guilt, and revenge. And it starts with a house party at Macbeth's castle. By the end, people are seeing ghosts, scrubbing away at invisible spots of blood on perfectly clean clothing and doing other crazy things. My insides froze as I remembered that strange look I'd seen earlier in Grandma Kay's eyes. But no. She couldn't be some kind of schizophrenic criminal who wanted to be caught—

"Jen?" Mark asked. "Hello? Are you okay?"

"Yeah, fine." I sat up straight and focused my eyes on his face.

"You made a really weird noise," he said.

"Kind of like a pig," Bri added helpfully.

I rubbed my face with my hands. "Sorry. I think I was half asleep. I stayed out too late last night. And the night before that. Graduation parties." I stretched my arms over my head and faked a yawn. It turned into a real one.

"Maybe you should go inside and take a nap," Bri suggested. "Mark and I are going to hang out in the garden. Your grandma said I could have some of my senior pictures taken back there this Friday, so I need to check it out."

Obviously Bri was still used to having things her way. Well, not tonight. I wasn't about to let her have Mark. Not that *I* wanted him, of course.

"No. I'll be okay." I smiled back at her.

"Super. I'd love to hear what you think." Bri stood up. "Of course, the photographer will have lots of great ideas. He's the best around."

And he probably was. The Harrises could afford it.

"You know," Bri went on, "My friends Monica and Lauren are going to keep me company during the photo shoot. Maybe you could come along, too."

"Oh, that would be great," I lied, "but I'm sure Grandma Kay will have a hundred things for me to do before the mystery weekend starts. Maybe I can take one of my breaks when you're here."

As we walked around back, Bri babbled about the six changes of clothing that she'd picked out so far. And that didn't include her pommer's uniform or riding outfit. It was beginning to sound like the photo session would take most of the day.

"What do you think?" Bri kept asking as she draped herself on benches and against trees. But when she slid her legs through the tire swing and wrapped her fingers around its thick rope, her question changed to "Push me?" Naturally, her blue-green eyes were focused on Mark.

He grabbed the tire on either side of her waist,

pulled it back, and then sent it flying forward. Bri's long blonde hair streamed out behind her like she was a model in a perfume commercial.

"Ready for an underdog?" Mark asked a few seconds later.

"Okay," Bri answered. She tightened her grip on the rope.

Mark got a good hold on the tire when it reached the highest point of its arc. His feet thudded as he ran forward. He extended his arms all the way up before ducking his head and letting go.

"Whoo!" Bri shrieked as if she were on one of the rides at Six Flags.

"Not bad," I murmured as Mark came over to stand beside me. "You almost got her up to Batman height."

Mark grinned at my use of our old tire-swing code. "Yeah, but it wasn't hard. She's really light."

"Now that you've got her going, what's next?" I asked. "Batman versus Joker with a twist?" That was our wickedest combination push. Batman meant going as high as possible. The Joker meant swinging around in a big circle. But it was the twist that gave the combo its extra punch.

"No," Mark said. "I'm pretty sure Bri would puke her guts out."

Ha. That didn't sound like something a guy would say about someone he wanted for a girlfriend.

"Mark!" Bri protested. "Come on, push me again!"

"Hold on," Mark said, running back over.

Then again, maybe I was wrong about that.

CHAPTER 6

Songs always seem to get stuck in my head when I'm running. During the cross-country regional last fall, bits and pieces of Queen's "Bohemian Rhapsody" kept repeating over and over during the last mile. It had actually helped. I finished in the top twenty-five—far better than I expected—and set a new personal record.

But on my first morning at the Schoenhaus, I kept hearing a variation on an old grade-school chant during most of my four-mile run:

> Bri's alone
> sitting in a tree.
> P-O-U-T-I-N-G...

I was breathing hard when I reached the driveway of the Schoenhaus. I'd stopped training after the regional meet because our long-distance coach said it wasn't a bad idea to take a week or two off at the end of the season. Plus, I'd needed every second to study for finals. But I could tell that I'd lost a lot of conditioning. My thigh muscles felt like they were made of cement by the time I reached the porch. The petals of the white roses were covered in dew.

I wanted to sit down on the front steps right there next to the rose bushes, but I knew if I didn't cool down, I'd feel it tomorrow. I did some Frankensteins along the sidewalk to the back of the house. Arms stretched straight out, I kicked my feet up to touch my fingers. When I got to the garden, I spotted Grandma Kay sitting alone in the sunroom with her fingers wrapped around a cup of coffee. Tuesday was usually the staff's only full day off. One set of guests had left by Monday at noon. The next group wouldn't show up until Wednesday at four o'clock. But this Tuesday would be a workday. I'd seen the long list of chores Grandma Kay had drawn up in order to get the Schoenhaus in perfect shape for her mystery club. When she caught sight of me, she slid open the nearest window and called, "Ready for breakfast?"

"As soon as I finish stretching," I told her.

"I'll scramble a few eggs," she said. "And how about a cafe mocha?"

"Sounds great," I said. "Thanks."

About five minutes later, I joined Grandma Kay in the sunroom. We talked a little about where I'd been running and what the weather was like outside. Finally, I decided to ask one of the questions that had hit me the night before. "You're not planning to actually catch a murderer or anything this weekend, are you?"

"No, of course not," Grandma Kay said. "I planned the mystery this year, so I don't get to play."

"That's not what I meant."

"Oh. You're talking about the other mystery, then. About your mother. Well, don't worry. The answer is still no. There won't be any kind of grand unmasking at the end of the weekend. I assure you, Jen, most of the people who are coming didn't even know Ellen."

"Most?"

"Well, Lynn, Steve, Barbara, Doug, and I all knew her, of course," Grandma Kay said.

I recognized a half-truth. They were my specialty. "Anyone else?"

"Oh, Ally Harris probably met Ellen a few times."

"And?"

"Goodness, you sound just like your father."

That wasn't an answer. I stabbed a piece of sausage with my fork, popped it into my mouth, and started chewing. Silence seemed to work for Dad. He must have learned his technique from Grandpa David because Grandma Kay sighed and said, "Okay. I wasn't going to warn you about this until Friday afternoon, but...an old friend of your mother's is coming."

I straightened. "Really? Who?"

"I'd rather that it be a surprise—for both of you."

"Why?"

"Because I, um, may have left her with the impression that I never talk about Ellen."

Well, *that* didn't surprise me. Until last week that's how it had been with the whole family. "But she might know something," I protested.

"Exactly! And I'm hoping that this mystery weekend is going to make her subconscious start working overtime. She and your mother were college roommates and then colleagues at the same accounting firm. All the characters for this weekend are based on people Ellen used to tell me about."

"So how is this supposed to help?"

Grandma Kay sighed. "That's what Barbara wanted to know, too. But trust me, Jen. I know what I'm doing. And once we wrap up the mystery weekend, all three of us will sit down and talk about what happened in real life. Okay?"

"Maybe," I said. "If you'll just answer a few other questions."

"Like what?"

"Well, you told Uncle Doug that there were a lot of things going on the day my mother left. I was wondering what they were."

Grandma Kay sighed. "Let me start just a bit earlier, so I can put everything in context for you. The last time I saw your mother was the Saturday before she disappeared. Everything seemed fine between her and your dad. Perfectly fine. Sure, they hadn't been able to spend much time together for a while. But things are always crazy at the end of a semester."

"Yeah," I agreed. Dad and I usually ate a lot of frozen pizza during finals week.

"Then your Grandpa Roger was planting the roses out front on Monday afternoon after all the guests had left. When I went to check on him, he was sitting on the front steps with his head in his hands. He admitted to feeling dizzy. But he told me not to worry. Missouri clay is horrible stuff, and digging in it is hard work. Besides, it was the first really hot and humid day that spring. Of course, I wanted to take him to the emergency room. But he insisted that he'd be fine. He had a doctor's appointment the very next day, so he kept saying, 'Why pay doctors twice when it's probably nothing?'"

"That sounds like him," I said.

"Stubborn old man," Grandma Kay said. "But at least I stopped him from tackling any more yard projects that afternoon. And it was a good thing, too. The next day—the day your mother left—he had a heart attack in the examining room. If it had happened out here, he probably would have died."

I tried to imagine what life would have been like without Grandpa Roger. He was the one who babysat Mark and me during the year that I'd spent out at the Schoenhaus. And later, he'd taught me how to hit a softball, shoot a layup, and play cribbage.

"Yes," Grandma Kay went on, "it could have been very bad. The first person I called after Steve was your mother. I knew she'd come sit with me. This will sound like a cliché, but she was like a daughter to me. Even if your father hadn't been proctoring final exams, I probably wouldn't have called him. He has a devastating talent for saying all the wrong things in hospitals. I had learned about that years earlier when your Grandpa David had his stroke. But your mom didn't answer the phones at either her office or your house. I didn't find out until the next day that she'd disappeared without a word. I should've known that she wouldn't have done that."

"But Dad said she'd left him before."

"Yes, she did. Once. And you know what? She came straight here." Grandma Kay tapped her index finger on the table. "Your dad was extremely stressed over grad school, and he was taking things out on her. Not very nice. Not very nice at all. I was extremely angry with him. So your mother and I decided it would be best for him to sweat it out for twenty-four hours."

"Really?"

"Yes. And that time, she did at least leave him a note. I suppose running to your mother-in-law for help sounds a bit backwards. But Ellen had left home right after she graduated from high school and never looked back. Your other grandmother, may she rest in peace, had a lot of problems. I think that might be one of the reasons that the police didn't pursue things any further. They thought it was a family pattern."

"So the police were involved, too?"

"Of course they were. Your dad filed a missing persons report when Ellen didn't come home. He was afraid something might have happened to her. Her car turned up in a tow-away zone near one of the big hotels down by the Arch. The police didn't find any fingerprints, fibers, or DNA that shouldn't have been there. So the police thought she must have...."

"Must have what?"

Grandma Kay sighed. "Must have run off with someone. And I was a big enough idiot to go along with it. With Roger in intensive care, I just wasn't thinking straight. This probably sounds stupid, but I resented her for not being there when I needed her."

That didn't sound stupid at all. Not to me. I stared down at my plate. There were a few bits of scrambled eggs and half a sausage left on it. I wasn't hungry.

"The trail has gone stone-cold," Grandma Kay went on. "It's officially a closed case. I know that. But I'm determined to jog someone's memory this week-end—someone who might know something. And you actually have some evidence at home that we might be able to link to a murderer. After all, who else could have sent all of those letters?"

"Well," I said, "my mother *could* have sent them."

Grandma Kay nodded slowly. "That's a real possi-bility, too. But in that case, maybe the letters could actually help us find her. I would certainly love to be wrong about all of this. But if I'm not, wouldn't you be happier knowing the truth, Jen?"

I would've been happier if I hadn't had to think about my mother or her disappearance at all. But that wasn't an option now. "I guess so," I said.

"Good." Grandma Kay gave me a sharp nod and pulled a crumpled list out of her pocket. "We have plenty to do. The countdown is on to the mystery weekend!

CHAPTER 7

I collapsed into the garden hammock, wishing I could escape the Schoenhaus for a while after hours of sweeping, scrubbing, and dusting it. My muscles felt like I'd just been working out in the weight room. For a few minutes, I stared up at the green leaves overhead. They trembled in the light breeze. I wondered if I should drag the hammock out of the shade. Then I might finally be able to do something about my track tan. But it was too hot. Plus, I'd have a tougher time reading the book Uncle Doug had passed on from Lisa. I'd made it through the first hundred pages of *Crocodile on the Sandbank* the night before. The story had kept me from thinking about Grandma Kay's mystery until my eyes were ready to close on their own. I opened the book and found my place. Soon my mind was far away in Egypt.

"Working hard or hardly working?" a deep voice asked.

Annoyed by the interruption, I glared up at Mark. "Hey, I just got off work half an hour ago. You wouldn't believe the list of things Grandma Kay had for me to do."

"Actually, I think I would," Mark said. "What's that new perfume you're wearing? It's lemony fresh."

I swung at him, nearly falling out of the hammock. He easily dodged out of the way.

"Want to go for a bike ride?" he asked. He tapped the strap of his backpack. "I brought enough water for both of us."

"No."

"Lazy," Mark said.

"I already ran four miles today."

"Listen, Jen. I need to talk to you."

"About what?" I asked, my mind still on tombs, mummies, and handsome archeologists.

"Are you serious?" Mark asked. "Don't you remember what happened with Grandma Kay last night? I've hardly heard anyone say anything about your mom ever—and then *bam!* Everyone freaks out."

"Your dad seemed pretty calm."

"'Seemed' is the key word. He was sleepwalking again last night. He only does that when something's bugging him and—" Mark broke off as the back screen door slammed.

Grandma Kay descended the back steps, carrying two glasses.

"Great," Mark muttered. "I want to talk *about* her, not *to* her."

"Why?"

"Are you coming or not?"

"We can't go now," I answered. "She's brought us drinks."

Grandma Kay arrived, beaming. "Your timing is perfect, Mark. I had just finished making a pitcher of lemonade when I saw you."

"Thanks, Grandma." Mark took one of the glasses.

"Thanks," I echoed as she handed me the other one. The pale green glass was already dripping with condensation.

"So, what are you two doing?" Grandma Kay asked.

"We're going on a bike ride," Mark said.

Grandma Kay frowned. "Isn't it a little warm for that today?"

"It'll only get worse this summer," Mark pointed out.

"True. I'll push supper back to six thirty, so you won't have to rush home, Jen."

"Great," I said, still not moving.

Mark widened his eyes and tilted his head to the side in a clear sign that it was time for me to get up. I handed him my lemonade and swung myself out of the hammock.

"How far do we have to go?" I whispered as we followed Grandma Kay back to the house. "I'm really tired. I'm serious."

"Not far," Mark said.

Once we reached the Katy Trail bike path, my uncousin set out at an insulting crawl. I picked up the pace, passed him, and continued at a good clip for the next two miles. An evil and contented smile curved across my lips as I listened to Mark breathing hard behind me. He probably hadn't done anything more strenuous this spring than have fake battles with Gaston and waltz Belle around the stage.

A cooling wind blew against my face. Perhaps this idea of Mark's wasn't so bad after all. Then I heard a deep, ominous rumble over the continuous low popping sound that my bike tires made as they rolled over the trail's gravel. Thunder. I looked over my shoulder. A long line of dark, almost black clouds stretched across the horizon. Lightning flickered.

"I don't suppose you checked the weather forecast before you came over?" I asked, slowing down to let Mark catch up.

"No. Why?"

"Take a look behind us."

Mark stopped and turned around to stare at the sky. "Whoa," he said. "Not good."

"We'll never beat that back home."

"The Vinchgau is only a mile farther down the trail. We can make it to Barbara's gazebo before the rain starts."

"She'll be mad if I don't go in again," I said.

"We'll go in," Mark said. "Just not right away."

He pushed off. I let him set the pace.

One of the virtually unbreakable rules of track and field is never to look back. It wastes time and interferes with form. "Run your own race," my long-distance coach always insisted. "Don't worry about the runners at your back." Of course, the runners at my back never carried lightning bolts that they could throw at me if they got close enough.

We finally made it to the winery turnoff. Following

Mark's example, I leapt off my bike and pushed it up the steep, curving trail. Just as we reached the edge of the courtyard, the first few drops of rain struck the flagstones, leaving wet circles the size of a quarter.

Mark and I guided our bikes under the shelter of the gazebo and propped them up against the railing. Then we stood side by side and watched a curtain of rain sweep down the river bottoms. Lightning flashed to the south. I counted to eight before the thunder rumbled.

And suddenly we were caught up in an early twilight. Rain pounded on the roof. Only the dark wood of the gazebo and the deep green rhododendrons bordering the nearby woods managed to hold their color. Everything else took on a strange shade of gray.

Everything except Mark. His unruly dark hair stood up in tufts. His red T-shirt rose and fell with each breath he took. A dark rim circled the greenish blue of his iris. I had absolutely no business noticing the color of my uncousin's eyes. I shivered and looked away. The air temperature had dropped ten degrees in the space of a breath. The storm front must have been passing right over our heads.

"Cold?" Mark asked, turning toward me.

"A little," I said. "Let's move the bench out of the rain."

Together we slid it closer to the center of the gazebo and sat down. The rain drummed on the roof and pounded against the flagstones.

"I guess Barbara won't come out in this weather demanding to know what's going on," Mark said.

"We probably could've found a quiet corner somewhere at the Schoenhaus," I said.

"Yeah. But you know how Grandma Kay always turns up right when we don't want her to."

Mark was right about that. Even when we were younger, it didn't matter whether we were trying to steal a cookie or sneak into the forbidden storage area of the basement—she always caught us.

"So what did you want to talk about?" I asked.

Mark's eyes, with their suddenly fascinating rims of darkness, looked into mine. His brows had pulled together, leaving a small dent between them. "So let's say for a second that your mom didn't leave on her own. What else could have happened?"

I'd had plenty of time to ask myself the same question in the last few days. "Probably not suicide. Someone would have found her."

"Yeah," Mark agreed. "And if she'd had some kind of accident, it's the same thing. Besides, neither of those scenarios would explain why you got all that stuff in the mail—unless someone just thought it would make you feel better when you were little."

"But it did," I said. "Kind of. I used to love getting things from her. But the letters and presents stopped in eighth grade. I got a necklace for Christmas that year and that was it. No explanations. Nothing."

"Hey, I think I remember that Christmas," Mark said slowly. "You held up the necklace for a second and then you started to cry."

"I did not."

"Did, too." Mark's words echoed so many of our

former fights, but his tone was gentle this time. "You weren't bawling or anything. You had a cold that week, so when you blew your nose, everyone pretended not to notice. When you went to the bathroom, your dad said, 'Ellen should just stop it.'"

"Stop what?"

"That's exactly what Grandma Kay said. And then your dad said something like 'Ellen should stop sending things. Doesn't she know that she's hurting Jen even more? If she can't visit or at least call, she should just back off.'"

"I never knew that," I whispered.

Mark looked out at the rain. "I just remembered it myself. So I guess the question is, did word get back to your mother...or did word get back to her killer?"

I tried to think who might have been there that Christmas, but I couldn't be sure. Grandma Kay usually had thirty or more people over for dinner on big holidays.

"And there was never a return address?" Mark asked.

"No. The bigger presents were sent from catalogs or stores."

"Didn't your dad ever try to find her?"

"His lawyer hired a private detective before the divorce. Nothing turned up."

"I thought it was pretty much impossible for people to just disappear like that."

"Yeah." I hesitated for a long moment before continuing. "But I know Grandma Kay had an older theory."

"What was that?"

"She accused Dad of doing something to make my mother leave him."

"Someone actually told you that?"

I looked at my hands. "You did."

"No way."

"Did too," I said. My older self warred with my younger self for a moment. The hurt five-year-old won. "You said it right after you pointed out that you had two mommies and I didn't even have one."

Mark grimaced. "Really? I know I used to be a little jerk sometimes, but I didn't know I was that bad."

I shrugged. "You may have been getting back at me for painting pink flowers all over your camouflage tent."

"Now *that* I remember," Mark said. He hesitated. "So...what do you remember about your mom?"

"Nothing much."

"Nothing much is something."

"Everything is more of a vague image than a memory." I closed my eyes and tried to think back. "A soft voice at bedtime reading me books. Hands turning pages. Warmth. Fingers combing through my hair. Songs."

"What kinds of things did she talk to you about?" Mark asked in a smooth, level voice.

I tried to go deeper into my memory bank—to hear my mother's words and see her face. It had been so long that I'd almost forgotten what usually followed such attempts. A surge of panic rose up out my gut. I shut my eyes tighter. My muscles tensed. I tried to take a deep breath. All I managed to do was make an odd croaking sound.

"Jen, what is it?" Mark's hand gripped my arm just above the elbow. "Did you remember something?"

"No." I opened my eyes. His face was inches away from mine. Our knees and thighs were touching.

Mark let go of my arm and shifted several inches down the bench. "Really?"

"No. I didn't remember anything more. Only what I told you."

Mark's expression was unreadable. He was a pretty good actor. "All right," he said. "So you didn't remember anything else. But something's going on."

The world around me darkened. I didn't know whether it was from the storm or from lack of air. I leaned forward, rested my elbows on my knees, and pressed my forehead against my crossed arms.

Mark put his hand on my back. "Jen?"

"I'll be okay," I said in a choked voice, "in a minute." I tried to breathe slowly and evenly, but not too deeply. I didn't want to start hyperventilating. The rain drummed on the roof of the gazebo. It ran down its cedar shingles in torrents. I started to shiver. Mark's hand left my back and he reached down to unzip his backpack. There was a rustling sound and a moment later I felt him arranging his windbreaker over my shoulders. His hand returned to its old place on my back. I could feel its warmth through the layers of fabric. Lightning flashed again. I could see the brightness even behind my closed eyelids. I counted to five before the thunder cracked.

Finally I sat up and combed my hair out of my face. "Sorry," I said. "This happens sometimes when I try to remember her."

"No, I'm sorry," Mark said. "I shouldn't have pushed you like that."

"I've avoided thinking about my mom for years," I admitted.

"When you stiffened up like that, I thought you'd remembered something about the murder," Mark said.

"No. Just how my mother dropped me off at the babysitter's on the day she left. And then...no one came to get me." Another rush of remembered panic flooded into my stomach. I pressed my crossed arms against my ribs.

"Hey, shhh. It's okay." Mark rubbed my back.

I took a deep breath and held it for a second. If I got it all out now, maybe I wouldn't have to talk about it later. "All the other kids had been picked up hours earlier. And Miss Hannah kept trying to call all my emergency numbers. No one answered. I don't think Dad had a cell phone back then. Miss Hannah tried to act like she wasn't worried. But I could tell she was. Dad finally came," I said. "But Mommy never did."

Mommy? I hadn't used that name for her since I'd stopped asking Dad when she was coming home. Mark looked as freaked out as I felt, so I finished in a rush. "My dad would always say, 'You'll see her soon,' whenever I asked him about her. I finally just stopped asking."

"Whoa," Mark said.

"Yeah." I took a deep breath and exhaled slowly. "Sorry."

"Stop apologizing," Mark said. "This isn't your fault. I should have thought things through better.

But it's always been us against the grown-ups when they were keeping secrets. If I'd had any idea—" Mark broke off. The faint sound of a tornado siren cut through the air.

He stood up, grabbed me by the hand, and pulled me to my feet. "'Let's go. We have to get inside— *now*."

CHAPTER 8

A bell jangled as Mark yanked open the winery door. A gust of wind nearly blew it out of his hand, but he managed to grab it and slam it shut behind us.

Chamber music coming from the stereo speakers nearly covered up the sound of rain on the roof. Nothing had changed since the last time I was here.

A wine-tasting bar ran along the length of the room. Framed prints by Aunt Lynn hung on the brick wall. Bottles of red and white wine lay on their sides in racks. Books, stationery, postcards, jam, glassware, and knickknacks decorated the shelves.

Barbara appeared in the doorway to her office a few seconds later wearing her red Vinchgau apron. Her eyebrows lifted in surprise when she saw us, then pulled together when she focused on my face. "Jen, Mark, is everything okay?"

"Yeah," I said. "Except for the tornado sirens."

"Sirens?" Barbara repeated. "Oh my. I didn't hear anything." She walked behind the bar and turned off the music. The high-pitched siren wail barely cut through the thick walls. "Come to my office," she said. "I've got a TV back there."

Mark and I wiped our feet on the mat before crossing the wide, smoothly sanded planks of the oak floor. Barbara's desktop didn't have a paperclip out of place. The computer, printer, and router were turned off. A worn, yellowed paperback of a Lord Peter Wimsey mystery novel lay open. Tuesdays were always very slow.

Barbara picked up the remote and turned on the TV. A forecaster from one of the St. Louis stations was standing in front of a weather map, talking about a hook echo and counterclockwise rotations. We watched in silence for a few moments as she explained how the storm was moving northeast in a line between Gray Summit and Chesterfield. Those in a direct path of the storm, she said, should seek shelter immediately. Luckily, we were far enough north to be out of the worst of it.

"I don't think we need to go down to the cellars just yet," Barbara said. "But we'd better keep the TV on. What were you two doing out on a day like today?"

"Bike ride," Mark said. "We made it to the gazebo just as it started pouring."

"Ah," Barbara said. "So you've been here for a while." Her eyes flicked to mine again. I smiled back at her as if that was nothing out of the ordinary. "Well then," she went on, "how about a game of three-handed cribbage while we track the storm?" Without waiting for an answer, she opened up the cupboard under the television and pulled out a wooden board. "Grab a chair. We can play at my desk."

While Barbara shuffled the cards, I sent Grandma

Kay a short text to tell her where we were. She knew I was smart enough to come in out of the rain, but the tornado warning might worry her. Between deals, Mark got Barbara started on what all this rain would do to the grapes. All I had to do was smile, nod, and listen. As I concentrated on searching for pairs and runs, the knot of tension under my ribcage began to ease. By the end of the first game, I didn't have to think about every breath.

The meteorologist stayed onscreen, pointing at the various angry red splotches on the map as the storm moved into the St. Louis area. By the end of the third game, the tornado warning in our area had expired. But the rain was still falling. Once Barbara closed the winery for the day, she insisted on giving us a ride home in her delivery van. I didn't argue. My muscles felt like they were ready to fall off my bones.

When we reached the garage at the Schoenhaus, Mark pulled my bike out of the back of the truck for me, then lifted his out, too.

"I can give you a ride all the way home," Barbara told him.

"No, that's okay." Mark shook his head. "It'll only take me two seconds to cut through the back. Thanks for the ride."

"Thanks," I echoed.

"You're welcome," Barbara said. "Say hi to your grandmother for me, Jen. Tell her to call if she needs any last-minute help."

"I will," I said.

Once Barbara had driven away in her truck, Mark turned to me. "Are you okay now?"

"Yeah," I said.

He studied me as if he didn't believe my answer. I wasn't used to him treating me like some kind of fragile flower. Even after he or one of his friends knocked me down in a game of three-on-three basketball, he never asked me that question. He would just offer me a hand up from the cement.

I straightened my shoulders and lifted my chin. At that moment, I realized that our eyes were almost at the same level. That probably meant our lips would be, too. *No,* I thought. *Don't go there.*

"What?" Mark asked. The dent between his eyebrows appeared. "Did you remember something else?"

"No," I said.

"Do you want me to come in with you?" Mark asked.

No way. I didn't want to be in the same room with Mark and Grandma Kay until I stopped having these strange new reactions to my uncousin. I didn't like him that way. I couldn't. Even though technically we weren't related.

"No," I said again. "I'll be fine once I have a chance to chill out tonight."

"Good." Mark nodded once. "See you later then." He swung his right leg over the seat of his bicycle.

"Bye," I said, and watched him ride out into the light rain.

A few minutes later, I made my way from the Schoenhaus kitchen down the stone stairs to Grandma Kay's apartment. The center of each tread was partly worn away from over 120 years of use. At the bottom,

I reached a tiled hallway. The first door on the left led to Grandma Kay's apartment; the second was the entrance to the unfinished cellars. When we were kids, Mark and I had always wanted to play hide-and-seek there among the stacks of old boxes. And Grandma Kay had always declared it off-limits.

On the wall to my right, there was a six-by-fifteen-foot fresco that looked as though it could have been transferred intact from an Italian palace. But the painting was actually only thirteen or fourteen years old. Aunt Lynn had been thinking about trying some mural painting, and Grandma Kay had offered her a wall on which to practice. Grandma Kay liked to call the work her "Miche*lynn*gelo," but only when Aunt Lynn wasn't around.

At first glance, it was merely a group of men and women gathered around a table for a feast. They sat in clusters of three like the guests pictured in *The Last Supper*. But there was something wrong with the story. One woman appeared to listen in calm serenity, but she clenched a handkerchief in her right fist. A man whose head was tilted back in a laugh had a slightly panicked look in his eyes.

And the year I turned eleven, I'd noticed something else. The man on the end didn't really belong to the group in which I'd always placed him. He sat at a little distance from the others, but it was his expression that truly set him apart. A small, secret smile curved his lips. The satisfied look in his eyes said that he had set some evil plan in motion and it had exceeded all expectations. When I mentioned this to Aunt Lynn, her face had lit up.

"You saw that?" she'd asked. "Not many people notice him. My private title for this work has always been *The Trickster*. I didn't mean for him to turn out that way. But once he did, the whole composition changed. It's completely unbalanced. Luckily, no one ever sees that guy down there near the edge of the piece, so I decided not to worry about it."

I turned away from the fresco and opened the door to Grandma Kay's apartment. It used to be the servants' quarters, but Grandpa David had remodeled it completely when they'd bought the Schoenhaus.

"Hello," I called.

"I'm in the kitchen," Grandma Kay answered.

I walked past the coat closet and turned the corner. Bright lights reflected off the desert rose granite countertops and stainless steel fixtures. The great room was on the other side of the white kitchen cabinets. I wished I could throw myself face-first onto the deep cushions of the contemporary sofa, but Grandma Kay was lifting a steaming pot from the stove. Dinner was clearly ready.

"You're right on time," Grandma Kay said as she drained the noodles. "Go sit down. I'll be there in a few seconds."

A tureen of beef stroganoff and a salad crowded with onions, peppers, and croutons had already been placed between the two place settings. To the right of each plate stood a long-stemmed glass filled with a deep red liquid.

"Wine? For me?" I asked. That was something that only happened on holidays.

"Maybe just one glass. I know some people would

say that I'm contributing to the delinquency of a minor," Grandma Kay said. "But you're not a little girl anymore."

"I never was that little," I said.

"Maybe not, but now you're most definitely a young woman. Plus, I feel like celebrating. We're on track for this weekend. I was a bit worried for a while, but Lynn and Steve volunteered to take care of a few things for me last night. Did you have a nice time with Mark today?"

"Mmm-hmm,"I answered vaguely.

"He was up to something today," Grandma Kay said. "I could tell."

I shrugged. "I don't know about that, but he did seem to think I wouldn't be able to keep up with him on the bike ride."

"Silly boy," Grandma Kay said. "But there was something else, too. I'm almost sure of it."

I tried to think of a good way to distract her. "Hey, I didn't get a chance to thank you for the framed prom picture."

"Wasn't that a great shot?" Grandma Kay said. "I can show you some others after dinner."

"That would be nice. Even though"—I hesitated for effect—"Kent and I broke up."

"Oh, no. When? What happened?" Grandma Kay asked.

I told her. The acting advice from Leah's dad about not holding things in worked great. I didn't quite cry, but I let my vision get blurry. Grandma Kay forgot all about Mark.

When I finished telling her the breakup story, she

shook her head sympathetically. "You know, I think he might have been spooked by the idea of high school ending and having to go out into the world. And when he finally figures out what he lost, it'll be too late. Ha!" A slightly wicked smile crossed her face.

"Kent's a nice guy, Grandma Kay," I said.

"Of course he is," she said. "And I saw the way he hugged you after you lost in the district finals."

I smiled. Kent had come to all my home basketball games and at least half of the away games. He'd come to watch me run at a few track meets, too, and those are mind-numbingly boring events that take forever.

"How long were you two together anyway?" Grandma Kay asked.

"Since January."

We wound up talking about Kent for the next hour or so. That might sound like torture, but it wasn't. Not when the other possible choices were Mark or my mother. I didn't drink much of the wine with dinner, but I kept sipping from my glass after we had finished eating.

All of a sudden, I felt exhausted. When I hid the third yawn in a row behind my hand, Grandma Kay narrowed her eyes. "Tired?" she asked.

"A little," I answered. But the truth was, I could barely keep my eyes open.

"You should hop off to bed then. The first sitting for breakfast isn't until nine. No one wanted the earlier option. But I'll need you in the kitchen a half hour before that to help with last-minute preparations. We've got eight guests tonight in six different rooms. Not bad for midweek, eh?"

"It's great," I said. My head spun as I stood up.

Grandma Kay eyed me with concern. "Are you all right, Jen?"

"I'm fine."

"Oh, dear. The wine was a bad idea," Grandma Kay said apologetically.

"No. I'm great. Really. It's just been a long day."

"Good night, then. I'll give you a wake-up call in the morning, in case you sleep through your alarm."

I trudged up the three long flights of stairs. As I looked back over the day, it seemed like weeks since Mark had appeared beside the hammock. My phone chimed once. When I got to my room, I punched a few buttons to open the text message.

Landed safely.
Everything OK?
Lv, Dad

No. Everything wasn't okay. But there was no reason for him to come rushing back from his conference. I didn't want him to worry, so I hit reply.

All good.
Lv, J

Usually, I lie awake in the darkness for about twenty minutes after I turn off the light. But tonight I felt myself being pulled into blissful unconsciousness even faster than when I'd had my wisdom teeth out.

CHAPTER 9

The next morning I appeared downstairs at eight thirty sharp, wearing my uniform. Grandma Kay had a collection of these outfits—square-necked dark blue jumpers, white aprons, and puffy little white blouses—probably designed to make people think of German dirndls. The crisp white aprons were a nice touch. They didn't just protect the dresses from stains. They also gave the outfits a shape.

As I checked the breakfast room for the third time, a woman settled herself at one of the tables in a chair facing the windows. Despite the deep lines in her forehead and around her eyes, her dark red hair was untouched by gray. She wore a thick gold chain around her neck and matching pieces at her ears and wrists.

I knew the waitress routine, but I couldn't help feeling a bit nervous. Breakfasts at the Schoenhaus were such big productions. I picked up a covered basket of warm peach muffins and carried it into the breakfast room.

"Good morning," I said as I set the basket on the table. "Can I bring you some coffee, tea, or espresso?"

"You're not Maddie," the woman said.

I blinked at the unexpected reply. "Uh...no."

"She's always here during the week. Has something happened?"

"Um, well, sort of..." As I explained about the accident, the woman's eyes practically accused me of pushing Maddie down the stairs in order to get her job.

"And you are?" she inquired at the end of the story.

"I'm Jen." Somehow, my name came out sounding like a question.

"You're Kay's granddaughter?" The woman's tone warmed immediately. "My dear, I am Juliana Saunders. I've watched you grow up, in a manner of speaking. Kay has told me so much about you. And of course, I've seen many pictures of you. I should have recognized you right away. But you're so tall. Have you thought about being a model?"

I smiled and shook my head, my standard answer for nice older ladies who made that suggestion.

"Well, it is so good of you to help out your grandmother in her time of need," the woman continued. "Now, Jen, the girls should be coming downstairs momentarily. We all like those little pots of espresso. No one makes it like Kay!"

I went back to the kitchen and reported Mrs. Saunders's request to Grandma Kay. "The girls?" I asked. "Are they her daughters? Granddaughters?"

Grandma Kay grinned as she pulled the tray of fluted quiche cups out of the stove. "No. Just the group of friends she travels with. She and 'the girls' spend several nights here over the course of the year.

They come every fall for the foliage tour and Okto-berfest. In December, they're back to see Augusta by candlelight. Every spring and summer, they come to see David's garden blooming. They also play bridge marathons in the library."

All of the "girls" seemed delighted to meet me when I emerged with two of the stovetop espresso pots, which I had to keep refilling. Finally, after linger-ing at the breakfast table for more than an hour, they announced they were off for a stroll. Grandma Kay let me know that she could handle the two remaining guests on her own, so I dashed up the stairs, grabbed my cleaning supplies from a tiny closet, and unlocked the first room on the right.

The Vineyard Room overlooked Uncle Steve's prop-erty. The pale lavender wallpaper was a Victorian repro-duction featuring twisting vines and bunches of grapes. My eyes swept over the room, looking for smudges or dust on the massive, carved walnut furniture and the pale marble fireplace. Not a spot anywhere. When guests were staying over, one of the rules was "Never clean anything that isn't dirty." Mrs. Saunders and the girls obviously had neat habits. The bureau tops were empty. A copy of the Events and Attractions guide to the area sat alone in the center of the desktop.

After making the bed and using my carpet sweeper to silently scoop up bits of tracked-in lint and dirt, I moved on to the bathroom, where I wiped away the watermarks on the vanity and set out clean glasses. Since Mrs. Saunders and the women were staying tonight, I didn't have to scrub the tub and floors.

The Rose Room had almost the same furniture as

the Vineyard Room, but its fireplace was adorned with imported Italian ceramic tile and its windows over-looked the garden. I worked quickly to return the room to its former immaculate condition. Then I moved on to the Azalea Room and Hydrangea Room. I had just closed and locked the last door when I heard laughter floating up from the front entry. Mrs. Saunders and her friends were back. I decided to escape down the narrow back stairway that led to the kitchen. Grandma Kay liked to give guests the idea that elves cleaned their rooms while they were away.

When I peeked into the sunroom to see what needed to be done, I spotted Grandma Kay and another woman sitting at a table. I immediately recognized Maddie's thick, dark hair. Her right arm was covered in a cast from the base of her fingers to a few inches below her shoulder.

"Maddie!" I exclaimed. "Hi! How do you feel?"

"Better than I look," she said. "Thanks for coming, Jen. I felt so badly for leaving your grandmother in the lurch until you said you could help out."

"Hey, no problem," I said.

"Things really are coming together just fine," Grandma Kay agreed. "It's only Wednesday. We have Bri scheduled to come in tomorrow and Sunday, so we're in good shape. But Jen, look what Maddie brought for you." Grandma Kay motioned to the black fitted shirt and matching short skirt draped over the back of one of the chairs. A frilly white apron completed the outfit. "It's your costume for this weekend."

"Can't I just wear this?" I asked, motioning at my uniform.

"That will be fine for breakfast and lunch. But it'll be fun to have you in something a bit more formal for late afternoon and early evening. Setting the atmosphere is important at these events."

"But I'll never fit into it," I protested.

"Just try," Grandma Kay coaxed. "Maddie wore it in the old days when we used to cater wedding rehearsal dinners."

"I'm at least five inches taller than Maddie," I pointed out.

"But you have such nice legs," Grandma Kay said. "You shouldn't be afraid to show them off. Come on, Jen. Try it on for us now so Maddie can see how it looks."

Maddie winked at me.

"Oh, all right," I grumbled. I grabbed the outfit and went into the bathroom.

I don't know how I managed to zip up the back. The bodice was so tight that I could hardly take a breath, but so sturdily constructed that I knew it wouldn't rip. The hemline was at least seven inches above my knees. I smoothed the skirt and looked at myself in the mirror. The cut of the dress showed off what few curves I had. And after nine months of cross-country, basketball, and track, I had to admit that my toned legs looked pretty good.

When I got back to the sunroom, a third person was sitting at the table with Grandma Kay and Maddie. My stomach dipped oddly as I recognized the back of Mark's head. There was no point in telling myself that I didn't have some kind of weird crush on my uncousin. Not when my body was acting like a great big lie detector.

Grandma Kay saw me come in. "Ha, I told you it would fit," she said.

Mark glanced up to give me a quick smile of welcome. Then his eyes returned to me in a classic double take. He covered his mouth with his hand, but not before I saw his grin. He probably thought I looked ridiculous.

"Don't laugh," I ordered.

"Hey, I'm not," he said from behind his fingers.

"Of course he's not," Maddie said. "You look fabulous, Jen."

"Indeed you do," Grandma Kay agreed. "Doesn't she, Mark?"

Mark's eyes glinted. "Not too bad," he said. Then he dropped his voice down an octave for a pitch-perfect version of the Catwalk song: "She's too sexy for her dress…"

With a wordless cry of protest, I picked up a coffee cup and cocked it back behind my ear.

He raised an arm to shield his head, but I could still see his grin.

"That wasn't quite what I had in mind." Grandma Kay frowned at Mark before turning back to me. "Don't worry, Jen," she said. "The outfit is actually quite tasteful."

"Maybe," I said. "But I can't breathe."

"I never could breathe in that outfit either," Maddie said. But she had a wistful, dreamy look on her face, so I was pretty sure she wasn't trying to help me out here.

I crossed my arms. "I enjoy breathing."

Grandma Kay studied me for a few more seconds. I thought she might be about to change her mind.

Instead, she turned to Maddie and asked, "What do you think? Black panty hose?"

"I'd better go," Mark said, as if the conversation had suddenly become too much for his male sensibilities. He stood up.

"Thanks again for bringing the box over, Mark," Grandma Kay said. "And give Lynn my thanks for putting all of the folders together for the mystery weekend. That helped a lot."

"Sure," he said. Then he looked back at me. "Hey, some of the guys are coming for basketball tonight. Want to play?"

"Yeah. That would be great," I said. Being in a group with Mark sounded pretty safe. Surely I wouldn't find myself staring into his eyes during the game.

"All right. We're playing at my house around six."

"Great. See you then," I said.

Once he left, Grandma Kay said, "Good. Then it's settled. You'll wear this costume on Friday and Saturday night."

Settled? I guess it was. Otherwise, I knew Grandma Kay would hold out until she got what she wanted. Oh well. At least Mark wouldn't be there.

CHAPTER 10

A re we done?" Bri asked. I walked slowly around the bed in the Vineyard Room. The six pillows of various sizes were arranged properly. I didn't spot any wrinkles. Then I noticed a problem. "Your end doesn't look quite right." I twitched the corner of the duvet so that it fell from the mattress with the correct diamond-like shape. "Okay, good," I said. "You can clean the first bathroom. Use the pink stuff on the toilet, tub, and sinks. The blue stuff is for the mirrors, countertops, and floor. Don't forget to turn on the shower when you're cleaning the sinks and toilet. It's easier to clean the tub if you steam it first. Call me if you have any questions."

"Listen," Bri said, "I'll give you twenty bucks if you do all the bathrooms."

For a split second, I found myself calculating how many gallons of gas I could put in the Volvo for twenty dollars. Then I told her no in the firmest voice I could manage. "We'll take turns."

"But I've got my senior pictures tomorrow. You know what those latex gloves can do to your hands. I want to look perfect." She held up the backs of her fingers and waved her French manicure at me. "I couldn't reschedule my appointment. Please?"

Or maybe she hadn't even tried to reschedule so she'd have a good excuse to avoid doing the bathrooms. The suspicion must have shown in my face because Bri stiffened.

"Come on, Jen," she said. "It's not like I'm a total wimp. I mean, I've probably shoveled more horse manure than you ever will."

I sighed. How could she make an observation about mucking out stalls sound like a putdown? It seemed to whisper, 'You'll never be able to afford to have a horse.' And that was ridiculous because I hadn't really wanted one since I was six. What if Dad was right about Bri? Thirteen years was a long time ago. She hadn't said or done anything really awful to me this week. "Fine," I said. "You can do all the bathrooms the next time we work together."

Bri pouted. "Couldn't I give you the twenty instead? I mean, it's not like you care about your hands."

No. Dad was wrong. Bri was just the same as ever. I felt like stuffing my hands into my pockets so she couldn't check out my less-than-perfect cuticles. Maybe Bri hadn't changed, but I had. "Why are you even working here?" I demanded. "You don't need the money."

"Mom thinks a job will look good on my college applications," Bri said, rolling her eyes. "It's so stupid. She's always, like, 'Your dad and I can send you anywhere you want to go, honey, as long as you can get in.' It drives me crazy. She's on me all the time."

Yeah, I thought. *Having a mother who cares about you and wants you to be happy must really be rough.*

"I'm serious," Bri went on. "College is all she thinks about. I'm surprised she didn't start nagging you and Mark about it on Monday night. All of my other friends have gotten the lecture."

Other friends? I didn't think I qualified. But maybe Bri was offering a partial ceasefire. "Getting an early start on the essays is probably a good idea," I said. "But I need a break from thinking for the next week or two."

"You're lucky you can take one. My first drafts are due to my college consultant next week. It's sooooo stupid."

"Well, speaking of breaks, we're not on one right now," I said. "Time to get back to work. And I'll do the bathrooms today. No charge."

"Thanks, Jen." Bri smiled up at me. "We'll work something out. I promise."

"You can take care of hanging up the towels and emptying the trash in the bathrooms," I said. "That way we'll wind up finishing at the same time. Don't forget to look under the beds. You never know what you're going to find." I didn't think Mrs. Saunders and the girls would leave any nasty surprises behind, but still...

That set the pattern. We did the beds together. She dusted and vacuumed. I removed every streak and spot from the bathrooms.

"Wouldn't a mop be better?" Bri asked as she watched me finish washing the bathroom floor of the Azalea Room on my hands and knees.

I shook my head. "It doesn't work as well."

"And drying off the whole shower with towels?" Bri said. "What's up with that?"

"It's the only way to take care of streaks."

"Maybe by the end of the summer I'll have to take that Disney Princess quiz again," Bri said. "I might wind up being Cinderella. Not that you'd be, like, an evil stepsister or anything," she added quickly.

"Of course not," I agreed. We still had two bathrooms left to do, and I doubted Bri would want me to change my mind before I finished them. I stood up and did a final sweep of the bathroom. No dirt. No streaks. No spots. I pulled off my latex gloves and ran my hand lightly over the marble countertops and white porcelain sink. Smooth. That meant clean. The toilet paper had its special, pointed fold. Even Grandma Kay would be impressed.

"So anyway, I was wondering," Bri said. "Does Mark have a girlfriend?"

I shrugged. "He did this spring."

"And now?"

"I don't know. He hasn't said anything about her."

"When I was talking to him a couple of nights ago, he didn't say a word either. So maybe it's over," Bri said. She sounded hopeful.

"Mmm," I said, and promptly headed for the door.

"I had some people over for a bonfire on Tuesday," Bri continued as she pushed the vacuum cleaner out into the hall. "I would've called you after I called Mark, but he said you were totally wiped out and needed to chill."

Tuesday. The bike ride, the storm, the panic attack.

A slightly anxious feeling grew underneath my ribs, but I smiled and shrugged. "Yeah, I was really tired. I think I fell asleep before eight."

"Wow. Was everything okay?" Bri asked, her eyes wide with fake concern.

As if I would tell her anything. "Oh, yeah. I played basketball with the guys last night at Mark's house and felt fine."

Bri's eyes narrowed, but then she nodded in a pitying kind of way. "Good, because Mark seemed a little worried. Isn't his frown the cutest thing ever? By the way, he's coming over to go horseback riding with me tonight after dinner."

"Have fun," I said, as if I meant it. "Just be careful of your nails, okay?"

"Don't worry. I will," Bri said. "When do you think we'll get done today? I definitely need some time to get ready."

"We should be able to wrap things up before four," I said.

That should give her plenty of time prepare for a romantic horseback ride. Who cared, anyway? It was stupid to have any feelings whatsoever for a guy who'd like Bri—at least no feelings other than cousinly ones. Mark was just someone close to me who'd been there for me during a tough moment on Tuesday afternoon. I was glad the panic attack had happened with him and not Dad or Grandma Kay.

After Bri went home, I changed into a T-shirt and a pair of basketball shorts. Then I went through all the rooms one last time, inspecting them for flaws. Grandma Kay would do this herself, but I didn't want her to find any problems when I was in charge. The faucets gleamed. The wood shone. I couldn't find a crooked towel or a wrinkle in a bedspread on either of the two upper floors. All the downstairs rooms were clean, too. Since there weren't any bookings that night, everything would stay perfect until the first guests arrived for the mystery weekend.

From the sound of plastic crinkling in the kitchen, I could tell that Grandma Kay had arrived back from the store. I went to help her unload. While I carried the bags in from the garage, she stowed everything in its proper place.

"Bay leaves!" Grandma Kay groaned when we finished emptying the last few bags. "You haven't noticed any bay leaves, Jen?"

"No."

"How could I forget bay leaves? They're absolutely essential for the soup on Saturday. Drat!" she exclaimed. "I don't want to go all the way back into town. And they don't always have what I need at the local market. Would you run over to Steve and Lynn's? They probably have some."

"Sure," I said, even though I really didn't want to see Mark right now. I didn't want to be reminded of his big "date" tonight.

I took a shortcut through the backyard. Not a breath of wind stirred the hot, humid air. It pressed against my skin like the wrappings of a mummy. I opened the gate that led from the Schoenhaus garden to Uncle Steve's vineyard. It was several degrees cooler among the vines. Clusters of grapes hung from them like bunches of tiny green rubber balls.

My heart thumped as I heard footsteps behind me. I stopped and turned around, slowly and casually.

An older, shorter, and bulkier version of Mark stood there: Uncle Steve. It looked like he hadn't shaved since Monday night. His hair was damp, rumpled, and uncombed after a long day of work. His limp T-shirt had a snag on the right shoulder. I suddenly remembered what Mark had said about his dad sleep-walking again on Monday night. But when I looked into Uncle Steve's eyes, their expression was clear and warm.

"Hey, Jen," he greeted me. "Are you here to shoot hoops with Mark again?"

"Uh, no. Grandma Kay ran out of bay leaves. She needs them for the soup on Saturday."

"We have some in the kitchen," he said. "Lynn or Mark should be around. Otherwise, walk right in and grab them."

"Thanks."

"You're welcome," Uncle Steve said absently, as if his mind had already returned to something else. He turned down the next row of grapes and moved slowly away.

A few minutes later, I reached the old brick farmhouse where Grandpa Roger and Uncle Steve had grown up. I went around to the back door and knocked. It swung open and Mark stepped back to let me in. "Hey, what's up?" he asked.

"I need some bay leaves for Grandma Kay."

"I'll look."

He walked across the pale linoleum floor to the gas stove. Then he opened a cupboard door and spun a lazy Susan in circles until he spotted the right container. As he handed it to me, his fingers brushed against mine.

"Thanks," I said, backing away.

"How's Grandma Kay?" Mark asked. The look in his eye told me this wasn't just a polite question.

"Pretty normal," I said.

"Good. How about you?"

"A bit stiff from basketball, but otherwise fine," I said.

"Hey, the guys are coming over again tomorrow night," Mark went on in his normal voice. "Can you play?"

I shook my head. "I'll be cleaning up after the mystery dinner, but I might come over to work on my jump shot tonight."

"Sorry," Mark said with an apologetic smile. "I'm busy tonight."

I'd been thinking about basketball, not Bri. But now that their date had come up, it seemed like a good idea to admit I knew about it in case Bri said something later. "Oh, yeah. That's right," I said. "Bri mentioned you guys were going riding."

"Yeah, she was getting a group together at the bonfire," Mark said.

I wondered whether Bri had managed to uninvite the other people. Or maybe they'd been in on the setup from the beginning. Should I warn him? No, my more sensible half decided. Mark was a big boy. He could take care of himself.

CHAPTER 11

When the kitchen door of the Schoenhaus opened the next morning, I could hardly recognize Mark through the tears that blurred my eyes.

"Jen, what is it?" He crossed the room in three long strides.

"Onions," I said, sniffing.

"Oh." Mark stepped back out of my personal space.

I grabbed a paper towel and wiped my eyes. "The first guests will start arriving in about five hours," I said. "Grandma Kay thinks we're right on track."

Mark's nose twitched. "Well, you *were*. I'm afraid we've got a problem."

"What's going on, Mark?" Grandma Kay asked as she entered the kitchen from the hallway.

"Lynn has some kind of stomach flu," he answered. "She was up all last night, puking her guts out. This morning, she could barely make it from the couch to the bathroom and back without falling down. Dad wanted to call, but Lynn wouldn't let him."

Grandma Kay's face softened. "The poor thing. She doesn't want to let me down. But it would be foolish for her to come tonight, even if she does get to feeling better. I'll think up some kind of excuse to call her. Do you need any ginger ale? I picked some up for the weekend."

Mark shook his head. "No thanks. We've got plenty. And Lynn hasn't even been able to keep that down yet."

Grandma Kay shook her head and then addressed the ceiling in a thoughtful tone: "Someone will have to take over Lynn's role. After all, the house party is supposed to be in her honor. But things will fall apart if I have to make too many changes..." Her voice trailed off. Her gaze slid down from the ceiling and came to rest on me. I'd seen that look before when she needed someone to weed the garden or make a fourth at pinochle.

"Wait a minute. I'm Helga the maid," I protested.

"Don't worry," Grandma Kay said. "I've already called someone to help me out with cleanup tonight. Everyone will understand the casting change. And then we'll need someone else to play the love interest. After all, Steve is far too old for you, and he'll want to keep an eye on Lynn tonight anyway. So..."

Mark was also familiar with The Look. He backed toward the door. "Oh, no. I have lots of work to do today."

"Sure, right next door," Grandma Kay said. Her eyebrows twitched. "Remember, I'm related to your boss. And since he's on the mystery weekend board, I'm sure he'd let you off."

Yep. Uncle Steve would do that.

But me pretending to be engaged to Mark? Having a good excuse to sit close to him, stare into his eyes, and lightly touch his arm? No. I definitely could *not* do that. It would be too weird. And what if Mark guessed how I really felt about him? That would be on the other side of awkward. Not just for this weekend, but for the rest of my life.

"You'd better find someone else to take over for Aunt Lynn," I said. "You know I can't act."

"Oh, you'll be just fine," Grandma Kay said. She tilted her head and gave me a crooked smile. "Especially for this part."

At that moment, I knew in my gut that Aunt Lynn had been assigned the part of my mother. The victim.

No. There had to be someone else to play this role, absolutely anyone else.

"What about Bri?" I cut in, my voice a few steps higher in pitch than normal. "She can act. And she likes Mark. Not that she's in love with him or anything. But he went riding with her last night. They'd be great together. They'd have so much fun." I turned to Mark. His cheeks had turned a deep shade of red. "Wouldn't you?"

"No." Grandma Kay shook her head. "I have every confidence in you, Jen. You'll be perfect."

"Jen will be perfect, but I'm busy," Mark said. "My buddies are coming over for basketball tonight."

Grandma Kay said nothing for a long moment. Mark crossed his arms and looked more stubborn with every passing second.

Finally, Grandma Kay shrugged and turned to me.

"Very well. Maybe Kent would help us, Jen. You two are still friends, right?"

I stared at her in horror. This was beginning to feel like one of those long-running, disaster-filled, early-morning nightmares. "Well, yeah, but—"

"Good. You can give him a call the second after I get off the phone with Lynn."

I felt panic setting in. How much more embarrassing could this get? Grandma Kay was making it sound like a big coed slumber party. While I frantically searched my brain for a good way to put a stop to this, Mark came to my rescue.

"How do you think that'll look to the guy?" he demanded, glaring at Grandma Kay. "They just broke up."

"But if I explain the situation—" Grandma Kay began.

"Forget it," Mark growled. "I'll take the part."

"Marvelous!" Grandma Kay exclaimed. "You'll have fun, I know you will. The mystery starts promptly at six. Dinner is at seven. Mark, you'll need to wear a coat and tie. Jen, that dress you wore to prom would be perfect. I don't suppose you brought it with you?"

To clean toilets? I shook my head, still speechless.

Grandma Kay sighed. "And nothing I have would fit you. You'll simply have to drive into town to pick it up."

Mark frowned. "All that way for a dress?"

"And shoes," Grandma Kay said. "Setting the proper atmosphere is important. We're all dressing up tonight. The clothes will help Jen project a certain image. Plus, while she's there, she can pick up some letters and envelopes that we talked about. This is as good a time as any to make the trip. Then we can go through all the evidence after everyone else leaves. Now you know how St. Louis rush-hour traffic starts before three on Fridays, Jen. So we'll need to make sure you get on the road soon. But first—"

"I have to get to work," Mark interrupted. "You can plan the rest of this without me, right? So maybe you could just give me my character notes?"

"Of course. I'll get your part printed up right away." Grandma Kay headed purposefully for the basement stairs.

"Whoa," Mark muttered as her footsteps died away. "She is totally psycho about this weekend. Otherwise she would never have thought about getting that Kent guy involved and—" Mark stopped and looked at me in shock. "Oh, man. She's having you play your mother, isn't she?"

"I think so. But the character can't really be my mom. The story's completely made up."

Mark stared at the basement door. "What is she thinking?"

"There's someone coming this weekend who knew my mother," I said. "I don't know who. But I think Grandma's trying to jar that person's memory or something."

"Oh," Mark said. "That makes a little more sense, then. Sort of. But this is still just too weird. Bri would do it. If you want me to, I could talk her into it."

I was sure he could. And she would probably sparkle in the part. As the maid in my stupid, skimpy costume, I would have to see them together. There were no good options. But I knew it would be next to impossible to change Grandma Kay's mind now.

"No," I said finally. "I think I'd better do it, but thanks. So did you guys have fun last night?"

"Yeah," Mark said.

Before he could say anything else, we heard footsteps on the stairs. Grandma Kay emerged seconds later, holding sheets of paper in both hands. She thrust the thicker stack at me and handed the other to Mark. "These are your character sheets. They describe who you are and how you should interact with the other characters. Everyone is using his or her own real first name to make things easier. Mark, as Jen's new fiancé you won't be expected to recognize anyone anyway, so if you wind up learning everybody's name tonight, that'll be just fine."

"Good," Mark said. "By the way, I work at the bike rental place on Saturday."

"And I know that boss, too," Grandma Kay said brightly.

"Don't even go there," Mark said in his deepest voice.

"Fine." Grandma Kay sighed. "We can say that you're off sulking somewhere."

"Good. So I was never here, right?" Mark said.

"Of course you weren't, dear," Grandma Kay said. "Don't worry. I know just how to handle Lynn. She won't suspect a thing. And I'll find some way to make all of this up to you, I promise. And Jen, the weekend won't be as bad as you think. See you tonight, Mark."

My uncousin made a face. "Great. Bye."

Once Mark had left, Grandma Kay turned to me. "Fortunately, everything's under control here. The rooms are ready. The table is set. The vegetables are chopped. But we'll need to spend some time working on what you need to say to everyone. You can start looking over your part while I call Lynn."

I leaned against the counter and began to read, but Grandma Kay's performance on the phone distracted me. As her voice moved from shocked disappointment to reassurance, I couldn't help listening. The suggestion that I cover Aunt Lynn's part sounded completely spontaneous.

But Grandma Kay's confidence in my acting skills didn't extend to my helping her trick Aunt Lynn. She covered the mouthpiece with her hand and announced quietly, "I'm pretending to ask you if you'll help. She doesn't suspect a thing."

"And you didn't tell her a single lie," I said, giving her an admiring look.

"Of course not. I never lie. Well, actually I do occasionally, but only when there is some higher moral obligation at stake. Or to be polite."

Grandma Kay shook her head as she took her hand off the receiver. "Jen agreed to do it. She's delighted. Now, I insist that Stephen stay with you. If he came, he would spend the whole time worrying.... What? Yes, you're right. He would be too old for Jen anyway.... Mark? What a wonderful idea! Can I speak to him?... Oh, right. I'll call his cell phone. Don't worry about a thing. I'm sure I can get him to agree. Just take care of yourself. If you're feeling better tomorrow, you and Stephen must come over. I have plenty of ginger ale and crackers on hand. And I have this wonderful Jell-O recipe...."

At that point, Grandma Kay started giving Aunt Lynn detailed advice on what, when, and how much to eat, so I started reading again. I already knew the general outline of the mystery weekend from my small part as the maid. But as the victim, I had to know absolutely everything so I could spend the evening sharing possible motives.

A little after one o'clock, I was on my way to St. Louis. My head was stuffed full of names, motives, and seemingly harmless phrases that were supposed to drive someone to commit a fictional homicide. I didn't know enough about my mother's life to figure out any parallels between her and the plot. I did guess, though, that the law office in the mystery was a substitute for the accounting firm she used to work for.

Traffic wasn't bad until just after the exits for Interstate 270. It started slowing down and then came to a complete stop. I drummed on the steering wheel nervously. This was taking too long.

I switched on the radio station in search of information. One announcer finally said that there had been a four-car pileup. An ambulance was at the scene. I picked up my character sheets and held them against the steering wheel so I could glance at them as I inched forward.

An uncomfortable feeling in my stomach grew as the minutes on the car clock advanced while the mileage on the odometer did not. Now I would have to fight rush-hour traffic to get back to the Schoenhaus. Dad was always complaining about St. Louis commuters. I wondered for a second what he was doing. Then I remembered that he was supposed to have given his paper this morning at the conference. Dad had made me promise never to text while I was behind the wheel, but traffic was close to a dead stop. Keeping an eye on the car in front of me, I punched in a quick question about how his presentation had gone. I probably hadn't moved a hundred feet when his answer came back:

Great! Good questions after.
Lv, Dad

Ten minutes later, I accelerated away from the wreck, feeling guilty. What was an inconvenience for me was apparently a tragedy for someone else. It was well past three by the time I stopped in front of the one-and-a-half-story brick house where I'd lived most of my life. Not a single dandelion was visible on the neatly mown lawn. Geraniums bloomed in twin planters of on either side of the steps. The yews and other shrubbery had been shaped and trimmed. Dad's love of order usually didn't extend past the front door, but he always tidied up the yard before we went out of town. He said that otherwise you might as well put up signs on the telephone poles giving thieves your address and travel plans.

I left the car in the driveway and hurried to the front door. After unlocking it and pushing it open, I closed it and tossed my keys on the small table in the entryway.

When I reached my room, I flicked on the overhead light. The comforter was halfway off the bed, the sheets all wrinkled. Half a dozen paperbacks cluttered the nightstand. My clothes lay in piles. I still hadn't straightened up my desk after finals week. Some people are born to be neat. Others have neatness thrust upon them—like working as a maid at the Schoenhaus. I was definitely in the second category.

I knelt beside the bed and reached for an unfinished pine box that I'd hidden on one of the slats holding up the box spring. Wood whispered against wood as I slid out the container. I set it on the bed and lifted the lid for the first time in years to reveal a stack of letters. My heart contracted oddly as I saw the words "Dear Jen," at the top of the last letter I'd received from my mother. I didn't dare read any further. Every second that went by, traffic was getting thicker.

A thought occurred to me: I should find another sample of my mother's handwriting, something that was undeniably hers. I scanned my bookshelves for my baby book. It was sitting on the shelf above my desk. The dates for my first tooth, first words, and first steps had all been recorded—and not by Dad.

When I opened the book, I saw that the first pages were dedicated to the baby shower. I ran down the list: Grandma Kay had given a high chair, Aunt Claudia had brought a playpen, and a woman named Dorothy Adler had made a quilt by hand. I smiled. That quilt was undoubtedly the one that I had folded away in the bottom of my sweater drawer despite the fact that it was falling apart.

I dropped the baby book beside the letters on the

bed and went to the closet to get the rest of the cards I had kept. My eyes fell upon the plastic garment bag that held my prom dress. I'd almost forgotten that it was my original reason for coming into town today. I grabbed it and threw it on the bed, then turned back to the closet. I knelt down and reached back into the right-hand corner for the brown paper grocery bag filled with the envelopes and cards. My grasping fingers touched the back of the closet and then the side. Nothing. Finally, I pushed my clothes out of my way to reveal a swirling collection of dust bunnies. The bag was gone.

The hangers squeaked in protest as I swept the line of clothes into the opposite corner. Still nothing. I looked up at the neat stacks of boxes on the shelf over the rod. Was that how I'd left them? I couldn't remember. Dad had threatened to clean out my closet for years. Had he decided to make a start on it when I was gone?

I dug through my entire closet in the hope that Dad might have just moved things around. But I couldn't find the bag or its contents anywhere. He couldn't have thrown it all away. Not without my permission. Right?

I ran downstairs to the garage and checked the recycling bins. Empty. So was the trash can. Well, that made sense. Garbage pick-up was early Tuesday morning. I rushed down to the basement to look on the shelves where Dad used to hold my toys for ransom when I'd left them lying around. But I only found a few half-empty cans of paint and a carefully folded drop cloth.

For the next fifteen minutes, I roamed through the house checking counters and cupboards until only one room was left. When I was little, it had been drilled into me that I was never supposed to go into Dad's room without permission. The old taboo held for a moment. Outrage won out. I looked under his bed and behind the dark green curtains. Nothing.

Next, I moved on to the tall oak dresser. I rummaged through the drawers of socks and underwear and sweaters without bothering to straighten up after myself. I was making a statement as much as a search: You went through my things; I'm going through yours.

In the bottom drawer, I came across an old cotton shirt I'd never seen Dad wear. The fabric was so thin that you could almost read a book through the blue, green, and yellow plaid. When I started to tuck it back in the drawer, some sort of paper crinkled in the pocket. Curious, I pulled out a faded yellow stickie and recognized the handwriting on the note right away:

Jerry,
   Two weeks until the end of tax season. Just over a month until the end of school. Then we'll breathe.
               All my love, all the time,
               Ellen

I dropped down on the bed. The man who had saved this note could not have thrown away my cards. At least, not on purpose. My anger faded abruptly, leaving me trembling with the extra adrenaline that my body no longer had any use for. When had my mother written this? It was impossible to tell. Who would put a date on a love note?

I caressed the paper with my thumb. Dad had kept that note in that shirt pocket for all these years. Why? What had my mother's disappearance done to him? Unlike Uncle Doug, he hadn't gone through a long series of girlfriends. To my knowledge, he hadn't had any girlfriends at all, although it is possible that he dated a few women here and there without telling me. The only female friends of his that I ever met were his safely married colleagues and some of his graduate students. But even those women had only appeared at the house in mixed groups for a holiday party or barbecue.

I didn't think Dad hated women. But his mother drove him to distraction, his wife had left him, and his daughter...well, I'd given him plenty of trouble through the years. He couldn't understand why I was so stubborn about some things and so laid back about others. How different would things have been if my mother had stayed?

Slowly, I slid the note back into its place, folded the shirt, and carefully returned it to the drawer. But I didn't have time to clean everything else up now. Dad would definitely notice that someone had been digging around in his things. I would have to confess when he got back.

Dad's closet was the only place that I hadn't looked. I decided to check it out just to be completely thorough. Grandma Kay would be sure to ask if I'd searched everywhere. I found a wide cardboard box wedged into the left front corner of the closet under a line of Oxford shirts. Inside it was a stack of hardcover blank books.

I opened the one on top and looked at the inside front cover. There, on a rose-covered bookplate, was my mother's name. On the line below, she had written the date—the year she had disappeared.

I stared at the familiar handwriting on the first page. The cursive was slightly messy and uneven, very different from the writing in my letters and the baby book. But that made sense. The pre-calc notes I scribbled in class always looked a lot different from the math homework I turned in. I sat back on my heels and began to read:

April 21

All of the parenting magazines talk about the importance of ritual in a young child's life. Jen has added something new to our routine. I always read her a story and sing "Stay Awake." When I finished a few nights ago, Jen announced that she was afraid of bears. I told her not to worry because bears lived outside.

She nodded wisely, looking a little like Jerry when he's going on about some new economic theory, and said: "Bears can't open doors."

So now, exactly four seconds after I finish the song, Jen starts the following nightly dialogue:

Jen: I'm afraid of bears.

Me: Bears live outside.

Jen: Bears can't open doors.

She's so serious about it that I've begun to have visions of a big brown shaggy creature lumbering up our back steps. It reaches its paw out for the latch and then stops with the sudden realization that it can't open doors.

For an instant I thought about trying to reach back and remember this ritual for myself. No. Bad idea. I turned the page.

Then the doorbell rang. A fist thudded against the door and a voice called my name.

CHAPTER 12

I dropped the journal, bolted out of my father's room, and thundered down the stairs. By that time, Leah had let herself in. She stood on the rug by the door. Her arms were crossed. "How long have you been home?" she demanded. "You could've called me."

"I'm just here to pick up a few things." I tried to sound casual, but my voice shook.

Leah frowned. "What's wrong? You look like you've seen a ghost or something."

"Or something," I said. My breath caught oddly in my throat as I inhaled.

"You need to sit down. Come on." Leah grabbed my arm and dragged me into the living room. She practically pushed me down onto the sofa and then sat down in a nearby chair. "So what's going on?" she asked.

For a second, I thought about lying. But then I knew I had to tell Leah the truth. Maybe she could tell me I wasn't going crazy.

"I just found my mother's old journals," I said.

"Wow," Leah said. "Where?"

"In my dad's closet."

Leah's eyebrows lifted.

"I thought he might have taken something that belonged to me," I explained.

"What?"

"A bag. It had all the cards and envelopes from my mother."

"But why would your dad want that?" Leah's frown deepened.

I shrugged. "Dad's been complaining about my closet for years. I thought maybe he decided to clean it out while I was gone. It would've looked like a sack full of trash to him, not important evidence."

"Evidence for what?"

Oops. I hadn't meant to say anything about that. But Leah was my best friend. I took a deep breath. "Grandma Kay thinks someone killed my mother fourteen years ago."

Leah gasped. "You mean, all those letters and presents and things—they weren't from her?"

"They might've been," I said. "But Grandma Kay doesn't think so."

"Who sent them, then?" Leah asked. "And who mur—I mean, why...?" Her voice trailed away.

"I have no idea," I said, sighing. I told Leah about Grandma Kay's theory and filled her in on everything that had happened at the Schoenhaus since Monday. Except for the parts about Mark.

"Maybe," Leah said slowly, "someone came and took that bag of stuff after your dad left. This is totally creeping me out. You can't go back to your grandma's, not with so much strange stuff going on. We'll think of some excuse for you to stay at my house."

"I can't. Grandma Kay needs a victim."

"She needs a *what*?" Leah squawked.

"A victim for the mystery dinner," I explained. "Aunt Lynn got some kind of stomach flu, so she can't do it. I'm playing the victim tonight and the maid tomorrow."

"That sounds even worse. We'll call your grandma and tell her that you're sick, too."

"I can't do that to her. She's counting on me."

"But what if—" Leah paused. "This is so wild I can hardly believe I'm about to say it, but what if your grandma has really lost it? I know your dad is always worrying about her...you know...her mental state. But what if this is the real thing? Or even worse, what if *she* killed your mom? One part of her could want the truth to come out. The other part wants to destroy the evidence."

"No!" I said. "Give it a break, Leah. That's just too weird."

"Not after you've taken AP Psych. We studied some pretty strange cases."

I remembered how I'd barely made it to my bed on Tuesday night before I fell asleep. Could Grandma Kay have put something in the wine?

"No," I said, both to Leah and myself.

"Okay, maybe not," Leah said. "But Jen, you don't really want to go back out there, do you?"

I didn't. I wanted to go next door to Leah's house and have her lie to Grandma Kay on the phone while I made loud barfing noises in the background. But I couldn't forget the grateful look on my grandmother's face when she promised that she'd make it up to Mark and me.

"I have to go," I said finally. "Besides, what could happen? The Schoenhaus is going to be crawling with people. So don't worry. Everything will be fine."

"Everything had better be fine," Leah said. "Text me with updates, okay? Otherwise, I'm skipping out on the volleyball tournament and coming out there. Got it?"

"Got it," I said.

"Good. Will Mark will be around? Maybe he could be a backup."

"Yeah, he'll be there. In fact, the poor guy got stuck playing the victim's fiancé."

"No way." A slow smile spread across Leah's face. "Wait a sec. He's not the real reason you want to go back, is he?"

"Of course not," I said. "He's my cousin, remember? Sort of."

Leah lifted one eyebrow. "It's not like you're really related."

"Yeah, well, it would still be incredibly weird."

"So it sounds like you've thought about this." Leah grinned.

"You know, I really don't need this right now."

"Probably not." Leah glanced at the clock on the fireplace mantel and sighed. "I should get back home. Devon will be picking me up for the tournament any second. In fact, she could be sitting in my driveway right now. The whole team is staying in a hotel tonight."

"Well, good luck. This is your last tournament before Nationals, right?"

"Yeah. I still wish I could drag you along. But if you change your mind, go to my house. If no one's home, there's a key in the third hanging planter from the left. Okay?"

"All right, thanks. But I'll be fine."

Leah's cell phone vibrated once and she checked the screen. "That's Devon. I've gotta go. You're going to text me, right?"

"Yeah," I said. "And you can send me your scores. Kill the ball a few times for me, okay?" I led the way to the front door and watched her sprint across my yard. Once she climbed into Devon's front seat, I exhaled with relief. I didn't want to go back to the Schoenhaus, but I had to. I didn't need Leah trying to talk me out of it.

As I climbed the stairs, I wondered what to do about the box of journals. Dad must have gone through them when my mother left, looking for clues to where she had gone. But just because he hadn't found any clues didn't mean they weren't there. I needed to read them myself. And maybe the journals would make up for the missing cards and envelopes. I went back into Dad's room and shut all the drawers. Nothing looked suspicious. But once he opened them... I decided to think about that later.

The journal lay where I'd dropped it. I wanted to see what else my mother had written about me. But there wasn't time. If traffic was really bad, I might not make it back to the Schoenhaus before six. That's when the mystery was supposed to start.

Since atmosphere was important to Grandma Kay, I decided to change now so I could walk onstage looking the part. Within a few minutes, I'd kicked my shorts and T-shirt under my bed and slipped on the prom dress. Its hem brushed the floor. I jammed my feet into my black heels. Then I went to the bathroom and looked in the mirror. There wasn't much I could do with my hair at this point, so I just brushed out all the tangles. Most of my makeup was at the Schoenhaus, but the lipstick, eye shadow, and blush that I'd bought for the prom were still sitting on the bathroom counter.

I grabbed them and stuffed the baby book and the letters into the box that held the journals. Since I was always wobbly in high heels, I went down the stairs slowly and headed toward the front hallway. My eyes were still on my feet when I opened the screen door. I gasped when its edge nearly caught Kent in the forehead. His hand was poised in front of the doorbell. My ankles chose that moment to collapse.

Kent grabbed my wrist for a second to steady me. His eyes widened slightly as he noticed my dress. The last time he'd seen me in it was in this exact spot after a final good-night kiss. He'd been wearing a tux instead of cargo shorts and a T-shirt.

"Hi," I said, feeling—and probably looking—like an idiot. I had to explain—fast. "I, um, have this party at the Schoenhaus tonight. Grandma Kay wanted me to get all dressed up for it."

"You look great," Kent said. With the grace of a guy in one of Grandma Kay's old black-and-white movies, he took a step back and pulled the screen door open all the way to let me out. "I was cutting through your neighborhood when I saw your car out in the driveway. And I kind of wondered how things were going for you…" He suddenly looked as embarrassed as I felt.

"It's all great," I lied as I pulled the front door shut and locked it. There wasn't time to go into everything that was wrong even if I'd wanted to. "The money's not bad at the Schoenhaus. And I like my boss a lot."

"Your grandma's pretty cool," Kent said.

"Yeah." I led the way down the steps and headed toward the station wagon.

"So what's the party for?"

"Oh, it's just one of Grandma Kay's mystery weekends. She has a club where they do this role-playing game once a year. Everyone has some kind of part to play—some reason to want someone dead. A person usually gets murdered on Friday night. Then everyone spends Saturday hanging out and looking for clues. On Saturday night after dinner, everyone except the organizer and the corpse write out their explanations for how and why it happened."

"Even the murderer?" Kent asked.

"I think the murderer writes out a confession, actually. They read everyone's theories in the library afterwards. From what I've heard, some of them can be pretty funny. Whoever has the best answer wins. If no one figures out the right murderer—or if the reasoning for correct guesses is all wrong—the organizer wins the Christie and the murderer takes home the Marple."

The right corner of Kent's mouth lifted in one of his familiar half-smiles. "So there's no credit for a right answer unless you show your work, huh?"

"Exactly," I said.

"It sounds like fun."

For a second, I thought about what this evening would've been like if I'd let Grandma Kay drag Kent into the murder weekend. But no. Mark was right about how weird that would be.

"Everyone has a great time, apparently," I said. "Unfortunately, I got stuck in traffic on the way here, so I'll be late getting back. I need to hurry."

"Hey, what's that?" Kent said suddenly. He took a few quick steps ahead of me and knelt beside my car. "Check this out," he continued, pointing to a puddle of oil spreading slowly across the ground. "You'd better not drive this baby anywhere but the shop."

"Oh, no," I whispered, horrified and hopeful at the same time. Bri might still be able to step in at the last second. And she probably had a closet full of dresses to choose from, even if she wouldn't have much time to prepare for the part.

"This mystery thing—it's that important?" Kent asked.

"Well, I am playing the victim."

"Don't you have an understudy?"

"I *am* the understudy."

"Okay, then. I'll drive you."

"Oh, thanks, Kent. But you can't. It's so far. And there's another girl Grandma Kay might still be able to get."

Kent shrugged. "I have time. Unless you'd rather not be stuck in a car with me for a couple of hours..."

"Don't be stupid."

"Good. But listen, even if it makes you a bit later,

we should at least blot up some of this oil first."

"True," I said, sighing. Dad wouldn't be happy about finding a gooey black mess on the driveway. The chaos I'd left in his dresser drawers was enough for one day.

"I'll do it. You don't want a bunch of oil spots on your dress. Give me your keys. You can wait in my car. It's open."

I felt like one of those useless girls from an old James Bond movie as I let Kent take care of everything. But he was right. Oil spots might never come out of my dress. After I sent Grandma Kay a quick text to let her know I was running late, I looked down at the box at my feet. I was dying to pull out one of my mother's old journals, but I knew this wasn't a good time. I took out my character sheets instead and started reading.

Kent handed me my keys and purse as he got behind the wheel. I was glad he'd noticed the purse on the passenger seat of my car because I'd forgotten all about it. It didn't match my dress, so I tucked it into the box and closed the flaps. We didn't say much to each other for a while as Kent dealt with the bumper-to-bumper traffic on Highway 40-61. He glanced down at the character sheets that I was studying.

"Tell me about the mystery," he said.

I read everything Grandma Kay had written about the setting, the characters, and the secrets, as well as the comments that I was supposed to insert into the conversation.

When I finished, he asked, "But who's going to be the murderer?"

"Grandma Kay wouldn't tell me," I said. "That's how the game is played, I guess. Or maybe she's afraid I'd give everything away if I knew. "

"Don't worry," Kent said. "You'll do great. Why don't you practice on me?" He made a prissy, puckered old lady face. "Please, Jen, darling, do tell us about your book. The character of Lana intrigued me so."

For the rest of the trip, Kent played the different characters in a variety of voices. I had to admit, I was beginning to feel much better.

As we drove into the crowded parking lot of the Schoenhaus, I saw a large group of people lounging on the covered porches. Their heads turned expectantly as our car slowed to a stop. The men wore suits; the women had on floor-length dresses of silk, satin, and chiffon.

"Looks like I'm not overdressed," I said.

Kent grinned. "Let's give them a show. You stay inside and leave the box where it is for a second. I'll open your door for you."

He jumped out and walked around the car. After opening my door with a flourish, he took my hand and helped me to my feet. He didn't let go of my hand.

"Thanks for the ride," I said. Even with the high heels, I still had to tilt my head back to look up into his eyes.

"No problem," Kent said. "I'm really sorry about your car, Jen, but I'm glad I happened to be driving by. I've missed you. A lot."

My cheeks burned. I didn't answer. I couldn't. I wasn't about to tell him I'd missed him, too, when I had no clue where he was going with this.

Kent filled the silence. "I've been asking myself for the last two weeks why I thought it was a good idea for us to break up."

"Because we've both got years of college ahead of us before we can really get serious about anyone," I reminded him, quoting his exact words.

"What was I thinking?" Kent shook his head. "But we can't talk now. The curtain's about to go up."

I glanced over his shoulder at the spectators on the porch. "It probably already did."

Kent squeezed my hand before letting it fall. "Guess we've given them something to talk about, huh? I've always wanted to be a red herring."

Grandma Kay came down the porch steps. "Jen, what happened? Where's your car?"

"The stupid Volvo decided to leak oil all over the driveway. Luckily, Kent was driving by and came to my rescue."

"Really?" Grandma Kay said. "Well, at least you didn't have a breakdown on the freeway. Kent, thank you for arriving on the proverbial white horse. I don't know what I would have done without Jen this evening."

"You're welcome," Kent said.

"Will you stay to dinner?" she asked. "We could work you into the plot."

"Thanks," Kent said, "but I have a softball game later tonight."

"Oh, that's too bad," Grandma Kay said.

He turned to go, then stopped. "Hey, Jen, we almost forgot your stuff." He ran to the car, pulled out the cardboard box, and ran back again. As he handed it to me, he said in a low voice, "Call me once you have your schedule for next week, okay? Maybe we can get together."

"Sure," I said. "And thanks again."

"No problem," Kent said. "Talk to you soon."

Grandma Kay beamed at Kent as he got back into his car. Once he closed the door, she whispered, "I couldn't have planned it better. You should have seen the look on Mark's face when you two arrived. He played the jealous young man to perfection. But I'm sure Kent would have enjoyed tonight if he'd stayed."

"Grandma Kay, we're not going out anymore," I reminded her.

"Right," Grandma Kay said. "Sorry, dear." She spun on her toes and headed back to the porch.

I followed reluctantly, conscious that everyone was looking at me. Mark and Uncle Doug stood at the top of the steps like two well-dressed, disapproving gargoyles. Mark was playing the annoyed fiancé, but I wasn't sure why the lawyer Uncle Doug was portraying would be so out of sorts.

According to Grandma Kay's original plot, the senior partner of the law firm was supposed to have a hopeless passion for the victim. But that story line had been designed for Aunt Lynn and the man who'd gone in for gall bladder surgery. Since that would have been extremely weird for Uncle Doug and me, Grandma Kay had promised to add a note to everyone's welcome folder to make him more of a second father to my character.

Mark looked downright gorgeous in his dark suit and red tie. I decided that it would be in character for me to check him out more fully. So I did. Mark's frown had deepened by the time I reached his face. But I kept smiling up at him as I mounted the steps.

"Hail to New York's latest literary lion," called a voice from the porch. "Will you remember us, Jen, when you're topping the *Times* best-seller list?"

I stopped at the top of the steps and studied the person who'd asked the question, a trim older man with a full head of wavy gray hair. I hardly recognized Jim Boyd, one of Grandpa Roger's best friends, in a suit.

"Of course, I'll remember you, Jim," I answered, although it felt very strange to call a man who used to give me piggyback rides by his first name.

"Besides," I continued, "you're the one who doesn't seem to remember me. I saw you at a cozy corner table at Garibaldi's last week with one of your clients. I waved, but you looked right through me."

Mr. Boyd shook his head. "Sorry, I haven't been to Garibaldi's in weeks."

"Well, if you were there, I doubt Jen would have talked to you anyway," Barbara said with a sniff. Her earrings jangled as she tossed her hair.

"Oh, don't be such an old stick-in-the-mud," Grandma Kay told her friend. "Jen promised that she'd show your new novel to her agent, and she will."

"Yes, but..." I hesitated in what I hoped was a condescending fashion. "Have you finished rewriting the middle chapters? The plot seems a bit muddled, and the motivations aren't clear."

"Plot? Motivation?" Barbara demanded. "I taught you the meaning of those words, young lady. Words fail me when I think of all the time I spent helping you to develop your gift."

I took an involuntary step backward at the malice in her voice. My toe touched the solid wood of the porch, but my stiletto heel pressed against empty air. I felt myself falling. Mark made a grab for me, but he only succeeded in knocking the cardboard box from my hands.

Strong fingers clamped around my left wrist and jerked me forward. Uncle Doug hauled me upright and then continued to hold up my arm as if he had just landed a prize fish. A horrible thought struck me. I had shaved my underarms that morning, hadn't I?

"What were you thinking?" Uncle Doug shouted without letting go. "Did you want to crack open your skull?"

"Ow," I said.

Uncle Doug dropped my arm. "Sorry."

"Don't apologize for saving me." I squinted at his face. It had turned an odd, pale color under his tan. "Are you all right?"

"Other than being almost frightened to death," Uncle Doug said. He sat down on the porch railing and glared at me.

Mark stooped down to pick up the box, which luckily hadn't opened. "Did you have a nice drive with your old friend?" he asked in a cold and resentful voice.

My high heels made it possible for me to look down my nose at him. "I'm lucky he gave me a ride," I said. "The Bentley was leaking oil and—"

"Oh, please," Mark said. "Old cars leak oil all the time."

"Ah, young love," Grandma Kay interrupted. "The two of you can continue your squabble during dinner, but for now, Jen, why don't you put your things up in your room?" Keeping her voice low so the others couldn't hear, she added, "Then you can help me take care of some last-minute things in the kitchen."

"All right," I said, relieved to have an excuse to make my exit.

That seemed to be the signal for everyone else to rise with offers of help. I left the chattering crowd behind and went up the stairs. But instead of putting the box in my room, I stuck it under a stack of sheets in the third-floor linen closet and locked the door. Then, clutching my purse in one hand, I headed for the back stairs.

An unfamiliar woman's voice rang out from behind me: "Ellen! You're the last person I expected to see here."

CHAPTER 13

llen? I spun around. But the hall was empty, except for me and the woman who'd just called out my mother's name. The stranger stared up at me with a horrified look. Her cheeks flushed. The pale skin above her square-necked, low-cut bodice suddenly turned all blotchy. But she stepped forward to meet me with her hand extended.

"Oh, no. I've really put my foot into it this time, haven't I?" she asked. "But you look exactly like your mother from the back. You must be Jen. My name's Dorothy. I was a friend of your mom's. We went to college together, and then we worked in the same accounting firm."

"Then...you must be the Dorothy who gave me a quilt when I was born," I said slowly. She had to be the old friend of my mother's Grandma Kay had told me about at breakfast on Tuesday morning—the surprise guest Grandma Kay had designed this mystery for.

The woman looked pleased. "I did make you a quilt. Your mom told you?"

"Your name is stitched into a corner of the backing," I said.

"Got it. Well, I certainly missed your mom when she went to New York. I always wondered how she liked her new job."

"Job?" I asked, startled.

"Yes. A week or two after she left, I got a call from some Human Resources person."

"Someone called?" I repeated, feeling like an empty-headed parrot.

"Yes. From another accounting firm, in New York, I think. I didn't catch the name. They wanted to know Ellen's work habits and all that. She did get the job, didn't she?"

"Um, I don't—"

"Never mind, sweetie. That was a long time ago. Sometime this weekend we'll have to sit down together so you can tell me what your mom is up to these days." Dorothy lowered her voice. "We'll just have to do it when your grandmother's not around. You see, I spotted Kay at the Women of Mystery lecture that the St. Louis Public library put on. I recognized her from the wedding, and I knew that she and Ellen always got along so well. Anyway, I went up to her, and she said in just the coldest voice I've ever heard, 'I don't discuss or think about Ellen.' Then she turned around and walked away."

"Oh," I said.

"It was awful. But it all worked out. Kay came up to me right after the talk and apologized. She explained that your mother was no longer in touch with the family. We chatted for a while about this and that and then she told me all about her mystery club. She even invited me to come check out the group this weekend. How could I say no?"

She couldn't. Not if Grandma Kay really wanted it.

"Maybe we can sit next to each other at dinner," Dorothy went on.

"I'd love to, but I think Grandma Kay put out place cards for tonight."

"Well, I guess I'll have to corner you later, then," the woman said. "After all, dinner is supposed to start in about two minutes."

"And I'm supposed to be helping," I said, glad to escape. "I guess I'll see you downstairs."

"Don't worry. I'm sure we'll find time," Dorothy said. "I'm looking forward to getting reacquainted with you. You probably don't remember, but we actually spent quite a lot of time together when you were little."

I could only paste on my best smile in response.

"In fact," Dorothy continued, "the very last time I talked to your mom on the phone, you grabbed it away from her so you could say hello."

"So you haven't actually spoken to her since she left?" I asked.

The corners of Dorothy's mouth drooped and she shook her head. "No. And it just makes me sick inside. Especially since your mom wanted to get together a few days before she left town. I could tell she wanted to talk about something."

"Did she say what?" I asked, trying to keep my voice smooth and calm. This could be exactly the kind of information Grandma Kay had been looking for when she set up this mystery plot.

"No. And then I had to cancel for some stupid reason that I can't even remember now. She said not to worry—that we'd get together later. But after she left like that, without even giving notice, I always felt that I let her down." Dorothy's voice wavered and fell silent.

"It's okay," I said.

Dorothy smiled at me, but her eyes were too bright. "No, it's not. But enough of that. This weekend is going to be a lot of fun. I have to say, though, for some reason the characters are giving me flashbacks about the people at the place where your mom and I worked. That bunch was even more dysfunctional than this crowd of characters, if you can believe it, with all the petty jealousies and backstabbing. I never dreamed there'd be so much drama in accounting. But I'd better let you dash downstairs and help your grandmother."

I dashed. At least I dashed to the door that led to the back staircase. Once I was safely on the other side, I clutched the railing and slowly made my way down the narrow steps. My ankles still wobbled in those stupid high heels. Worse, I couldn't help but be horribly aware of every single breath I took. I couldn't have another panic attack. Not now. What if I totally lost it at dinner with everyone watching? On the other hand, maybe that wouldn't be such a bad thing. Only Grandma Kay and Mark would know that it wasn't part of the scheduled entertainment.

When I finally reached the kitchen, Mark was the only one there. He said the perfect thing to make me feel better.

"If you'd wanted Kent out here," he snapped, "all you had to do was tell me."

All of my anxiety evaporated in a flash of anger. I slammed my purse onto the counter. "I *didn't* want Kent here. But I did need the ride. Seriously, the Volvo was toast—"

"And why did you try to make me think that he broke up with you?"

"Because he did," I insisted, raising my voice to match Mark's even though I didn't know what his problem was.

"You could have fooled me—not to mention all the other people out there on the porch. Everyone must think I'm a total idiot to be involved with you...with this."

"You're right about one thing," I said. "Everyone thinks you're an idiot. Especially me."

The kitchen door swung open and Grandma Kay entered.

Mark groaned.

My cheeks flamed. "Did anyone hear us?"

"Of course," Grandma Kay said, beaming. "Everyone did. Not all the words. Just the fact that you were arguing. Perfect. I couldn't have planned it better. You two are doing wonderfully. It sounded quite authentic. But hurry now. People are going through the buffet line. All the seats are assigned, so you'll have places next to each other. That way you can continue your little lovers' quarrel."

"Great. Just great," Mark said as he watched Grandma Kay leave. He glared at me again. "I hate it when she shows up like that. How did I ever let you drag me into this?"

"You volunteered," I reminded him. "And I used to be grateful."

I stalked out into the hallway. Grandma Kay's friends would probably consider it part of the evening's entertainment. Before stepping into the sunroom, I put on a smile. If it looked fake, that would probably be perfectly fine.

I got in the buffet line behind Bri Harris's mom. She was wearing a champagne-colored chiffon dress with beaded flowers decorating the bodice.

"Jen, you look absolutely gorgeous!" she said. "Where did you get that dress?"

I told her how I'd wound up buying it at a bridal shop near the St. Louis Galleria since most department stores didn't carry dresses that were long enough. Mrs. Harris shared what an extremely tough time Bri had in finding the right dress in a Size 2. Poor girl. Once we reached the end of the buffet table, Mrs. Harris nodded toward an empty corner of the sunroom, gesturing for me to follow her.

"I shouldn't be going out of character," she whispered, "but I have to ask. Was that Kent who dropped you off?"

"Uh, yeah," I said, surprised that she'd know his name.

Mrs. Harris smiled. "Kay told me about him when I came over to give her a hand this afternoon. Nothing too specific," she added quickly. "Just how you'd recently broken up with the very nice, very tall young man you'd gone to prom with. But after watching the two of you this afternoon, I couldn't help but wonder if you're back together now."

"Not exactly," I said.

"Well, it's probably just a matter of time, then. If he comes out to see you this June, you and Bri could double-date."

I kept my face blank. "Right. So, um, who is Bri going out with now?"

"Oh, nothing official, but you know Bri. Give it a few days..." Her eyes flicked back to the buffet table, where Mark was dumping a large scoop of mashed potatoes onto his plate.

"Ooh. Interesting," I said with what I hoped would sound like approval. Then I backed away.

I went straight to my seat. Mark sat down next to me without saying a word. Dorothy took a spot right across the table from him a few moments later. She raised her voice above the requests for salt, pepper, or butter and asked, "Your name is Mark, isn't it? Mark Lehrer?"

"Yes, it is," Mark said cautiously.

"I knew it!" Dorothy said. "In fact, I used to know your father well."

Mark blinked in surprise. "You did?"

Dorothy pressed her hand to her heart in an exaggerated gesture. "At one time your father and I were engaged to be married. And you are his very image."

"What?" Mark yelped.

"I meant that you look exactly like him, my dear. How well I remember those days in Central Park. We rode the Staten Island ferry together. And wandered through The Cloisters. But then our happiness was destroyed."

"Hmm," Mark said, in unwilling fascination. He must have finally realized that Dorothy was speaking in character. "Uh, what happened?"

"He was stolen away from me by someone like this two-timing tramp." Dorothy pointed at me. "Let me give you a piece of advice, young man: run away while you can. She will break your heart and bring you nothing but pain."

"I think Dorothy has a point, Mark," Mr. Boyd said, from a little further down the table.

My jaw dropped. For a split second, I wondered how Dorothy and Mr. Boyd could say such things about me. But this was all part of the game and everyone around me was waiting for an answer. I said the first thing that jumped into my head: "Mark has all my love, all the time."

As the words left my mouth, they sounded familiar. A heartbeat later, I remembered the note I'd found in my Dad's old shirt pocket. I tried hard to keep from shivering.

"We all saw you arrive," Mr. Boyd pointed out. "Didn't your ride know you're engaged?"

"Yes, of course," I said. "Kent was simply congratulating me on my engagement and wishing me the best. I'm just lucky he was in the neighborhood when my car broke down."

Grandma Kay cut into the conversation. "Jen, I've thought from your earliest drafts that your book was semiautobiographical. You're going to have to tell us who is who."

I shook my head. "I suppose you're all in it in some way, since a writer's work is the sum of her experiences. Except Mark, of course. I didn't meet him until I finished the final draft. And at that point, I don't think I could have fit him in." I hesitated for a moment as I thought of a way to get back at Mark for his unfair suspicions. "But in a way, he still made the book."

The whole table watched as I touched the back of my left hand to Mark's cheek and said, "I dedicated it to him."

Mark tensed as an appreciative sigh went around the table. But then he caught my hand and pressed it between the two of his.

"My darling," Mark said, in his lowest rumble. "No one else will ever know just how much that gesture meant to me." He pressed his lips to the back of my hand.

My entire body responded to his touch, even though I could see the glint in his eye. This was paybacks. My uncousin had always been the king of one-upsmanship. And with all his training in school plays, he was far more skilled at this kind of game than I was. He placed my hand back on the table and patted it.

"No public displays of affection at dinner," Grandma Kay said, but she sounded pleased. "So, Jen, you're not going to tell us who you used for characters in your novel?"

I shook my head. "As I said, most of you are probably in the book in some small way: a sentence, an opinion, a way of walking. But that's all."

"How can you say that?"

In an almost choreographed movement, everyone turned to look at the middle-aged woman seated near the foot of the table. Her dress had bright paisley ribbons sewn in vertical lines onto its black mesh fabric. The loud colors told me this had to be Beverly, the woman who'd held either the Marple or the Christie for the past six years. Grandma Kay had warned me to watch out for her. Now what was on her character sheet again? Before I could remember exactly what her problem was supposed to be, she let the whole table know.

"You can change the trimmings on a character: the height, weight, and circumstances. But you can't change the essence of the person. We both know who Lana is."

"Lana is a complete invention," I said stiffly.

Beverly leaned forward, her eyes glittering. "You deny that Lana is a thinly disguised representation of myself?"

"She must be a real horror or else Beverly wouldn't mind," Mr. Boyd remarked.

"No," Beverly insisted. "The character of Lana is the soul of the book. To steal someone else's soul for your own purposes is a heinous crime. And I intend to pursue it."

"I'm quite confident you don't have a case," Uncle Doug interjected in his role as senior partner. "There are no precedents to support that. There have to be facts, details, major similarities...."

"I'm sorry you feel this way, Beverly," I said. "Maybe we could sit down later and discuss it."

"Why? Are you thinking about a sequel?" Beverly demanded, then turned away with a loud sniff.

I shrugged and scooped up a spoonful of mashed potatoes. But inside, I felt a deep sense of relief. Dinner had just started, and I'd already brought out the motives for a few of Grandma Kay's major suspects.

"Pay no attention to her, Jen," Dorothy said. "Beverly always enjoys making a spectacle of herself."

People chatted for a while and traded a few barbs. But then a look from Grandma Kay told me I'd better get going on implicating a few other suspects. She had planted me in the middle of the table, so I worked my way into conversations on the left and right once I figured out who was who.

Grandma Kay finally tapped her glass. "As many of you know, my maid Helga had a family emergency. Fortunately, I have someone who'll come in to do the washing up later tonight. But I'd like a little help clearing the table so we'll be able to sit out here this evening. Do I have any volunteers?" She fixed her eyes on Mark and me.

The moment we raised our hands, everyone else did, too. I guessed that they already knew I was going to be the victim. So much for my attempts at acting.

"I'm sorry I was such a jerk before dinner," Mark said to me while I collected the matching burgundy placemats and napkins. "I think I started taking things personally, which is stupid."

"I know how it goes," I said. "Mr. Boyd sure did get me when he practically called me a two-timing tramp."

"That was kind of funny, actually." Up close, Mark's smile was almost overwhelming. "So how much oil leaked out of the Volvo?" he went on.

"Quarts," I said. Then I lowered my voice to a whisper. "And the old cards and envelopes were gone. I don't know whether I pitched them or someone took them."

"That's not good. Have you told Grandma Kay?" Mark asked.

"Not yet."

"Well, don't for now. We have to get through this weekend first. What was in that box? It was pretty heavy."

"My mother's old journals. At least that's what the book on top was...." I caught sight of Beverly's ribbon dress moving closer.

"This obviously isn't the place to talk about it," he said in an undertone. He leaned against me to whisper in my ear. "Meet me in the garden in five minutes, so we won't have an audience."

"We'll be followed," I whispered back.

"Yeah, but they'll give us more space than they would inside, especially if we seem to be on a romantic after-dinner walk or something." He grinned.

I nodded. The romantic part would be all for show. I carried the napkins and mats into the kitchen and dumped them in the pantry's hamper.

Grandma Kay clapped her hands. "Everyone out of the kitchen, now. We can leave the rest for later. Go on. We have plenty to do tonight. Thanks so much."

She grabbed me by the elbow as I was about to follow everyone else out. "Oh, dear me. I forgot all about the chocolates. Jen, would you get out a few of my cut-glass trays and arrange them?"

"Sure," I said.

Once the room cleared, Grandma Kay enfolded me in a hug. "This is turning out to be one of the best mystery nights ever, and it's all thanks to you. Never tell me that you're a rotten actress again. You and Mark were the only two people who didn't sound like they belonged in an old Danny Kaye movie. Such delightful films, but so overacted."

I smiled down at Grandma Kay as she let go of me.

"Now, don't take too long with the chocolate," she continued. "I have an interesting new parlor game for us to play." Then she left the room. I was halfway finished fixing the first tray when the door to the basement burst open.

"Jen. Thank goodness it's you," Mr. Boyd said. "I found something down there. You'll have to break it to Kay. I can't bear to do it myself."

An invisible fist squeezed my heart. For a split second I thought he might have found my mother's body, hidden away all this time. The storage areas of Grandma Kay's basement had always been off-limits. A shallow grave could have easily been concealed by stacks of boxes. But as I took a deep breath to answer, I realized that this had to be part of the mystery play.

"What is it, Jim?" I asked as I crossed the floor swiftly. "What did you find?"

"Follow me."

I kicked off my shoes, lifted my long hem, and followed Mr. Boyd down the stairs. When we reached the basement, the door leading to the cellars was ajar.

"This always stays closed," I said, trying to keep the panic out of my voice. I knew none of this was real, but I couldn't get rid of the uneasy feeling.

"I know. That's one of the things that brought me back here. Then I noticed something odd. Come on. We're almost there."

It wasn't until that moment that I recognized a false note in Mr. Boyd's voice, the tones of an inexperienced actor. Everything suddenly became clear. Like Mark, he wanted to talk to me without an audience.

Jim was the murderer. Not my mother's. Mine.

CHAPTER 14

For an instant, I wanted to turn and run—to save the poor, innocent character I'd played all evening. But that would be like Hamlet jumping into the audience and announcing that he simply wasn't going to go through with it this time.

I followed Jim—Mr. Boyd—into a large room lit by a single, naked bulb. The floor was hardened clay. Some of the plaster had flaked off the walls, revealing the bare stones and mortar. About fifteen labeled plastic crates, the kind Dad used for storing old documents and bank statements, were stacked in a pyramid in the corner. A large hand-lettered poster sat on top of the pile, proclaiming: "Congratulations! You have found the body!" On the floor, a single white rose had been laid in the middle of a chalk outline. This was the crime scene.

I shivered. "So Jim, exactly whom did I see you dining with at Garibaldi's?" I asked, still in character. "I thought your wife had forgiven you for your extracurricular activities for the last time."

"She has. And if you tell her what you know, I'll be cut off without a cent. I've always admired you, Jen, but—" Jim broke off with an evil laugh. "Did you suspect?" he asked in his normal voice.

"Not until twenty seconds ago."

"Great. Then maybe no one else does, either. Kay brought some of your things downstairs so you can hide out in her apartment until tomorrow morning. That's when you'll turn into Helga the maid, as I understand it. The blinds are drawn, so no one will see you. We might even be able to fool Beverly this time. Did you know that she wins the Marple practically every year?"

"I've heard. But I'm supposed to meet Mark in the garden right now," I protested.

Mr. Boyd frowned. "You two lovebirds have the whole summer to be together. Can't it wait?"

I opened my mouth and closed it again. *Lovebirds?* But explanations would take a long time. And I didn't want the whole party to notice the door I'd left open in the kitchen and troop downstairs to investigate. If Jim was caught standing over the "body," the whole mystery would fizzle out.

"I suppose so," I said. "But could you tell Mark why I couldn't make it?"

Mr. Boyd crossed his arms. "If I do, then he'll know I'm the last person who saw you."

"But he already knew I was going to be the victim. He's probably disqualified from guessing anyway."

"Honey, everyone knew you were going to be the victim. It couldn't have been any clearer if it had been stamped on your forehead. Please, Jen. This is important. He'll understand if you explain it to him later," Mr. Boyd said.

"Oh, all right," I said.

"Don't worry. I won't leave the poor guy alone in the garden. I'll grab a few innocent bystanders and we'll all establish a nice alibi together. Maybe the others will think it was a conspiracy. Wouldn't that be a coup?" Mr. Boyd chuckled. Despite the lines in his face and his gray hair, he looked like an eleven-year-old boy who'd just played a successful prank on the teacher.

He bowed and waved his hand toward the door. As we made our way back to the stairs, he turned off the lights behind us.

"Lock yourself in," he said. "Then no one will be able to peek in here, okay?"

"Okay," I echoed.

Grandma Kay had left several lights burning for me. My pajamas, a stack of paperbacks, and a note lay on the table. I picked up the note first, happy to see that Grandma Kay had printed it in big block letters instead of her usual scrawl.

IF YOU READ THIS, YOU SHOULD
BE SAFELY DEAD. TRY TO GET SOME
SLEEP. AND HELGA, DON'T FORGET
THAT BREAKFAST PREP STARTS AT
SIX.

LOVE, GRANDMA KAY

I placed the note back on the table and looked longingly at Grandma Kay's private door, which led directly to the gardens. I wanted to dash through it, find Mark, and tell him what had just happened. But we'd probably have an interested audience watching from the sunroom. This was a mystery, not a ghost story.

I turned off all the lights and peered through the blinds, my eyes searching for his familiar form. And suddenly it came to me. I'd fallen for him and everyone could tell, the same way Uncle Doug could tell I'd liked that green metal frog we'd seen last Christmas. But no one could give Mark to me for a late birthday present. And even if they could, I'd be tempted to hand him right back.

I rubbed my forehead. Things were complicated enough without me falling in love with my uncousin. Did he feel the same way about me? No, of course not. It was true that his behavior toward me in the last few days had changed, but that was probably because he felt sorry for me after I fell completely apart in Barbara's gazebo.

There was movement on the other side of the blinds. Mr. Boyd and Dorothy Adler were walking across the lawn toward the garden. Mr. Boyd waved to someone, but I couldn't see who. I turned away from the window, suddenly feeling very tired. If only my phone was down here instead of on the counter in the kitchen. Then I could send Mark a quick text.

Suddenly, I remembered my promise to Leah. She was expecting to hear from me, too. At least I could call her and let her know that I was safely "dead" in

Grandma Kay's apartment. She didn't pick up, so I left a message. Then I went into Grandma Kay's tiny spare bedroom to change. As I pulled off my dress, I felt as though I was peeling off the last remnants of the fascinating *New York Times* best-selling novelist. Grandma Kay had been right: clothes can change the way a person feels and behaves. Then I put on my pajamas, returned to the living room and its overstuffed sofa, picked up one of the paperbacks, and turned to the first page.

It didn't hold my attention. The least bit of noise from upstairs distracted me. After I found myself rereading the same paragraph three times, I gave up and rested the book on my stomach. I let my mind circle from the garden to the library to the linen closet, where I had hidden the baby book, letters, and journals. If only I could go get them to read.

A few hours later, the rasp of a key and the turning of a deadbolt woke me up. The strange, oddly vivid dream I'd been having fled from my mind as I sat up and gazed blearily at Grandma Kay.

"Still awake, Cinderella?" she inquired.

"Not exactly."

"One slipper would have been enough, you know."

"What?"

"You left your shoes in the kitchen by the back door."

"Oh, no. That's right. I kicked them off when Mr. Boyd said he had something important to show me in the basement. I didn't even think."

"It was wonderful. When I said how strange it was that you hadn't come with the chocolates yet, everyone jumped out of their chairs and headed to the kitchen," Grandma Kay said. "When we found your shoes, I was almost certain that Beverly would start baying like a bloodhound, pick them up in her teeth, and go bounding down the stairs. Instead, everyone dashed out into the garden and found Jim, Dorothy, and Mark sitting on some benches in the rose garden. But the best part of all was that half the people thought Beverly did it. She was alone in her room for a few moments during the crucial period. Ha!"

"You don't you like Beverly much, do you?"

"Of course I like her. We just have a very competitive sleuthing relationship, that's all. Now, before I forget, this is for you." Grandma Kay picked up a small, brightly wrapped package from the end table and handed it to me.

"You didn't have to get me anything."

"I didn't. It came in the mail for you today. The package was addressed to me or I wouldn't have taken it out of the envelope."

I picked at the tape with my fingernail. "I wonder who sent it."

"It had a St. Louis return address, so I figured it must have been one of your friends," Grandma Kay replied.

Inside a box of sturdy cardboard I found a smaller one covered in blue velvet. I lifted the lid to reveal a small pearl ring. The gold band curved like some elegant mathematical function.

I slid the ring onto my finger. It fit perfectly. So why did I have a sudden vision of it hanging loosely on a young child's hand? "Have I seen this before?" I asked, puzzled.

"Well, I certainly have," Grandma Kay said in a choked voice. "There's a note. You'd better read it."

I understood Grandma Kay's reaction as I unfolded the paper and recognized the familiar handwriting. I held out the paper so we could read the words together:

Dear Jen,

I always said this ring would come to you for your seventeenth summer. It should be a wonderful time, filled with the beginning of some things and the ending of others. My single biggest regret is that I could not follow your progress from a delightfully challenging toddler to a disarming young woman. If the day ever arrives when we come face to face, you will understand.

Mom

Understand? My eyes blurred with tears. There was no way she could ever make me understand why she'd made the choice she did. Could this note really have come from the same person who'd written that journal entry about my fascination with bears opening doors? But the handwriting looked the same and the voice was similar.

Ever since the letters stopped coming, I had refused to think of my mother as my mom. She hadn't earned that title. Moms were there in sickness and in health. They went to track meets, basketball games, and all-day volleyball tournaments. They didn't just...disappear. I looked up from the letter and into my grandmother's face. She stared blindly past me, her lower lip quivering. Then, without a word, she stumbled to the door. I didn't care that I was supposed to remain safely dead. I pounded up the stairs after her.

Grandma Kay raced to the paper recycling bin, dropped to her knees next to it, and started digging. Uncle Doug was staring at her with wide-eyed concern. Two pieces of bread lay on the counter behind him. He held a table knife in one hand and a jar of mustard in the other. He still wore his dark blue slacks, but he'd ditched his jacket and tie. His white Oxford shirt was open at the collar.

"What's going on?" he asked.

"I could have sworn I threw it in here," Grandma Kay said, ignoring Uncle Doug. She sat back onto her heels.

"Could it be in the trash?" I asked.

"No," Grandma Kay replied. She dug deeper. "Wait a minute. Doug, you might have seen it."

"It?" Uncle Doug repeated. "I still don't know what 'it' is."

"The package that I brought in from the mailbox this afternoon," Grandma Kay said. "It was in one of those heavy-duty padded mailer envelopes. Do you remember the return address or the postmark? Think, Douglas. This is important."

Uncle Doug's eyes rolled up toward the ceiling for a moment as he took time to consider the question.

Then he shook his head. "No. But I didn't really look at it. What's going on?"

"I could almost swear there was a St. Louis return address," Grandma Kay muttered.

"And that means...?" Uncle Doug asked. He peered over Grandma Kay's shoulder. I didn't have an answer. And even if I did, I couldn't have forced a word through the tightness in my throat.

"The package was to Jen from Ellen," Grandma Kay said. "A late birthday present for Jen. Ellen seems to have sent the ring she always used to wear."

Uncle Doug looked at me for confirmation. I nodded and silently held out my hand with the ring on it. "So that's good news, then," he began. He stopped and squinted at the pearl ring. "Are you sure it's hers? It does look a little familiar, but—"

Grandma Kay exhaled in disgust. "There was a note, Douglas. It was in her handwriting, and it said—it said..."

Alarmed by her change of tone, I glanced back at my grandmother. Her shoulders slumped and she pressed her right hand against her heart. Her breathing was fast and shallow.

"Aunt Kay!" Uncle Doug knelt beside her and put his arm around her shoulder. "Are you all right?"

"Don't worry, Douglas. I'm fine," she said in a low, flat voice. "I just realized what a wonderful job I'd done of fooling myself." With a grunt of effort, Grandma Kay slowly got to her feet. She walked to the sink, turned on the water, and started washing her hands in a slow, deliberate way. Her face was hard when she finally turned around.

"If Ellen doesn't want to be part of our lives, that's her choice," Grandma Kay said. "I've just been a selfish, nasty old woman."

"No," I said. I felt like ripping the ring off my finger and throwing it across the room. "No, you haven't."

"It's true. Deep down in my heart of hearts, I must have wanted her to be dead. What kind of person would hope for that? Just a completely evil and self-centered—"

"Stop it, Aunt Kay," Uncle Doug ordered.

"I've upset the whole family without the least bit of evidence." Grandma Kay turned to me. "And worst of all is what I've done to you, Jen. You've been so strong, but I could see in your eyes how much all of this has hurt you."

"Grandma, it's okay," I said. "And besides, what if—?"

"You're being way too hard on yourself," Uncle Doug cut in.

"No, I'm not. Both of you are being far too kind." But Grandma Kay's expression lightened. "At least one good thing has come of all this: I've put together a mystery weekend to be proud of. It's been a long, long day, and I'm going to bed. Good night." She spun on her toes and headed for the basement steps.

I opened my mouth to call her back, but Uncle Doug shook his head slightly. So I merely said, "Good night, Grandma. I'll be down in a minute."

Once I heard the door to her apartment close, I whirled to face my uncle. "What if my mother didn't send this?" I hissed. "What if her murderer did?"

"I suppose that is a possibility," Uncle Doug said. "But I'd rather your grandmother didn't think about that tonight. She'd tear the whole house apart."

"It's so obvious. The murderer is the only other person who would've had access to my mother's ring."

Uncle Doug nodded thoughtfully. "True. Except for your dad."

All the strength went out of my knees. I leaned against the counter to keep from falling. No. Not Dad. He wouldn't have done this. Hadn't Dad been the one who'd told everyone all those years ago that all the cards and gifts should stop? But what if Dad had been talking to *himself*? Had he thought it was a good idea at first to send me all those things so I would think I had two parents who loved me, but then somewhere along the line he'd changed his mind? And then, recently, he'd decided to throw the cards out? Could he have sent the ring, thinking that by pretending Ellen was still alive he would protect himself from murder accusations?

"Jen?" Uncle Doug peered into my face. "Are you all right?"

"Yeah. I'm okay." I took a deep breath and held it for a few seconds before letting it out. "We have to go through the trash. Tonight."

"We might want to wait 'til Sunday afternoon," Uncle Doug suggested, "when we've gotten rid of this crowd."

"No. Anyone who came into the kitchen would just figure they'd walked in on part of the mystery. Besides, do you know what the trash is going to smell like on Sunday?"

Uncle Doug wrinkled his nose. "You've got a point."

"I won't be able to fall asleep tonight if we don't do this. And Mark would come over and help us. I know he would."

"Okay. You're right. So here's the plan. First, we'll check out the recycling bin more carefully. That's where your grandma thought she put the envelope. If it's not in there, I'll go change and you can call Mark. But if we do find it, it would probably be best if you put the envelope aside until Sunday. Then we can check it against all that other evidence you mentioned on Monday night."

"That stuff's gone," I said.

"Gone?" Uncle Doug echoed. "Are you sure?"

"I'm sure. I checked everywhere."

"Is that why you were late this afternoon?"

"That and some other things," I said.

Uncle Doug's mouth twitched. Did he think Kent was one of those other things?

"So anyway," he said, "Aunt Kay might be awake, waiting for you downstairs. After we go through the recycling bin, you'd better pretend to go to bed and then sneak back up here."

I nodded.

"Good girl." Uncle Doug reached for the recycling bin and dumped it out. "We won't miss anything if we put it all back one piece at a time."

"Okay," I said.

It wasn't long before we'd put every scrap of paper and cardboard back in the bin without finding the mailer. Uncle Doug sighed and promised to meet me back in the kitchen after he changed.

I tiptoed down the basement stairs. When I reached the bottom, the Trickster seemed to look out at me from his spot on the far left-hand side of the fresco. *Do whatever you want,* his eyes seemed to say. *This is going exactly as I planned, and you can't stop it.*

I pressed my lips together to keep from answering. Who knew what people would think if they caught me arguing with a painting? I turned around and opened the door to Grandma Kay's apartment, trying to make just the right amount of noise so my grandmother would hear if she were listening for me, but not enough to wake her if she were already asleep. I turned off all the lights behind me as I made my way to the tiny bedroom. Standing in the hallway, I closed the door to my room. Then I held completely still for a moment and listened to the faint snoring from Grandma Kay's room.

Real or fake? I couldn't tell. But either was better than the fast, shallow breathing that had frightened me and Uncle Doug in the kitchen. I took a few noise-less steps down the carpeted hallway and listened again. Moments later, I reached the main floor and closed the door behind me. I looked around the kitchen for my purse. Someone had tucked it next to the four-slice stainless steel toaster. I quickly pulled out my cell phone and called Mark.

He answered in one ring. "Jen, you're alive!" he said in a voice of mock surprise.

"Actually, I'm dead. That's why I couldn't meet you in the garden."

"I figured. So what's up?"

"Grandma Kay got a package in the mail today, but it was really for me. It had a note in my mother's handwriting and a ring that belonged to her."

"Seriously?" Mark said.

"Yeah," I said. "But the mailing envelope it came in seems to have disappeared, so I'm about to check through the trash with Uncle Doug, just in case someone threw it out. Would you come help us?"

"Sure. But where's Grandma Kay?"

"She went to bed."

After putting my phone back in my purse, I went to get the big gray plastic bags of garbage from the rolling bin out back. Fortunately, the trash had been picked up, so most of the bags would be from today…or was it Saturday already? I hauled out all but the two white plastic bags on the bottom. I'd dumped them there myself on Thursday after Bri left.

To my surprise, Mark arrived before Uncle Doug did. My uncousin stood there under the outside light for a few seconds and watched me transfer a handful of mashed potatoes from a mostly full garbage bag into a mostly empty one. I had pulled on a pair of latex gloves to make the whole process a little less disgusting.

"Gross," he said.

"No kidding," I said. I didn't even want to think about what the glop would have looked and smelled like if we'd waited until Sunday.

"So where's the ring?" Mark asked.

I stripped off both my gloves and tossed them into one of the bags. Then I held out my right hand to Mark. He grasped it lightly and tilted it this way and that under the light to examine the ring. To anyone watching us, it might look like the gesture of a concerned fiancé.

The sound of creaking boards came from the narrow back steps. Mark let go of my hand. A few seconds later, Uncle Doug appeared in jeans and a polo shirt, carrying a couple of empty trash bags and more gloves. "Sorry," he said in a low voice. "That old busybody Beverly caught me on the stairs and started interrogating me. She's a scary lady. I barely escaped. Have you filled Mark in?"

"Sort of," I said. "He just got here, too."

"We can talk while we work then," Uncle Doug said. He reached for one of trash bags.

A little over a half an hour later, we were done. There was no sign of the mailer.

Uncle Doug studied the gray trash bags lined up next to the door. "You'd think it would have turned up."

"I know," I said. For a second, I felt tempted to go through all the bags again, but I knew there was no point. We'd all been careful. "Time to get these back in the bins, then. I'm sorry we dragged you over here, Mark."

"Don't be," he said. "It had to be done. Too bad we didn't find anything."

"I'll check through the basement trash cans tomorrow morning," I said with a sigh. "Just in case."

"Mark and I can finish up here, Jen," Uncle Doug said. "Are you going to be able to sleep okay tonight?"

"I think so," I said. "It's been a long day."

"See you at breakfast," Mark said.

"Don't you have to work?" I asked.

"Grandma Kay talked my boss into letting me come in half an hour late," Mark grumbled. "So I'll get to have even more fun with the mystery crowd. Lucky me."

"You *are* lucky," Uncle Doug said. "I'll be stuck with them all day."

"Good night," I told them both. As I pulled the covers up over my shoulders a few moments later, the weird dream that Grandma Kay's arrival had interrupted came back to me.

In the dream Dorothy, Leah, and I were wearing pajamas and having a slumber party in my messy bedroom back home. Dorothy, who seemed a lot younger in the dream, kept saying that someone else would be arriving soon. The person was late, but she was on her way.

And without having to ask, I'd immediately known: that person was my mother.

CHAPTER 15

"Jen, you've got to wake up," the voice said. A hand shook my shoulder.

I opened my eyes and lifted my head. "What is it?" I demanded. "What happened?"

"Nothing, at least not yet." Grandma Kay straightened. "We have to get breakfast ready."

I let my head fall back against the pillow. "Oh."

"You were very deeply asleep. I've been calling your name and shaking you."

Yesterday came flashing back. The missing bag. The journals. My talk with Leah. The ride with Kent. The mystery guests. The ring. Mark. The sight of Grandma Kay virtually falling apart.

I fumbled for the switch to my bedside lamp and flicked it on. Grandma Kay stood before me wearing chinos and an apron over a fine-gauge cotton sweater. Her silvery gray hair shone in the lamplight. Her hands were relaxed and peaceful, but a certain tightness around her mouth warned me not to refer to the events of the previous night.

That look was all the discouragement my cowardly heart needed. I decided to follow Uncle Doug's advice and wait until tomorrow afternoon to bring up any evidence theories.

"What time is it?" I asked.

"Quarter after six. Take a shower and get dressed. Then you can come upstairs and give me a hand."

Twenty minutes later, after I had dug through all the trash cans in the basement, I climbed the stairs. My hair was still damp. The scent of cinnamon rolls baking intensified with every step. When I reached the kitchen, Grandma Kay was ladling batter into muffin tins and humming "Here Comes the Sun."

"Sun?" I asked, seeing only darkness beyond the windowpanes. "What sun?"

Grandma Kay laughed as I squinted at the clock in the corner. "No. I didn't drag you out of bed at three o'clock in the morning, you suspicious child. It's still dark because a thunderstorm rolled through here about an hour ago and it's still raining. I have a feeling it's going to be one of those dreary, wet days. Fortunately, this group will keep busy looking for clues."

"What do you want me to do?"

"You can start getting the breakfast room ready. Work as quietly as you can. At eight o'clock, we can both start banging things about to rouse the guests. Breakfast runs from 8:30 until 9:30. A few early birds will arrive in a desperate search of their first cup of coffee of the morning before that, so try to finish up quickly. I want your first appearance in the sunroom as Helga to cause a sensation."

"Okay," I said, trying to match her bright tone.

From a closet in the corner of the kitchen, I pulled out a broom, a dustpan, and a plastic carrier full of cleaning supplies and went out to the sunroom. Cleanliness first, I decided, since I could always bring people silverware and plates as they sat down. I swept and mopped the tile floor before getting fresh white tablecloths out of the downstairs linen closet.

Then, swiftly and automatically, I set the table. Knives. Spoons. No forks. It was a continental breakfast today. Linen napkins with the simplest fold for breakfast. Sturdy china cups turned rim down. Plates. Sugar. But more than once I found myself blankly staring at a napkin or a spoon, unable to remember how it had come into my hand.

Every new train of thought that I tried curved back to my mother. Who had written the words and wrapped the package? If it really had been Ellen—my mother—that would just confirm the fact that she had abandoned and pretty much forgotten me for all these years. Maybe Grandma Kay was right. Maybe her absence would have been easier to take if she'd simply been dead all this time. But that certainly didn't mean I wanted her dead. The thought that her murderer had sent the ring to get Grandma Kay off the trail made me sick to my stomach.

Who else knew about Grandma Kay's murder theory? If I could believe Barbara, the list was very short: Dad, Uncle Doug, Aunt Lynn, Uncle Steve, Mark, and Barbara herself. Dorothy and the other guests were wild cards. I had no idea how much they knew. Of course I'd told Leah, but she couldn't have had anything to do with this.

I didn't even want to think about Leah's idea that Grandma Kay had lapsed into some kind of clinically deranged mental state and was orchestrating everything herself. After watching Grandma Kay manipulate Aunt Lynn yesterday morning and her mystery group last night, though, there was no question in my mind that she could do it.

But there was an even worse option. What if my dad had killed my mother all those years ago? Passion was always one of the classic motives for murder. He would have known how to sound just like my mother and what presents to send me. And once he found out that Grandma Kay was on the trail, he could have checked my room for evidence and destroyed it before he left for his conference.

It was all too horrible to even think about. So I got to work again and tried to keep my mind occupied with other things.

A few minutes after eight, I heard voices in the hall and fled into the kitchen.

"Someone's coming," I said.

Grandma Kay looked up from the bowl of fruit salad she was stirring. "Is everything ready?"

"Yes. Or at least close."

"Wonderful. I'm sure everything looks great. You can put the muffins in baskets while I bring out some coffee."

"All right," I said.

"And when you're done, sit down and have a cinnamon roll. From here on out, everything will be easy. You don't have to clean any rooms until the guests check out."

Grandma Kay left the kitchen with a coffeepot in each hand. I heard her greet people in the hallway. After I finished arranging the muffins, I sat down with a cinnamon roll. They were huge, bigger than my fist, and covered with vanilla icing.

"Can you believe it? Almost everyone came to breakfast early," Grandma Kay said when she returned with the empty coffeepots. "They're all afraid they might miss something. We may as well start serving. Give me a thirty-second head start, so I can see what everyone does when you walk through the door."

The reaction was everything Grandma Kay could have hoped for.

"Jen! Where have you been?" a woman exclaimed, half-rising out of her seat. I glanced over my shoulder before facing forward with my best puzzled look.

Uncle Doug's voice carried over the flood of questions: "I believe this is Helga, the new maid," he said. "We met late last night when she arrived. I was struck by the resemblance to Jen myself."

"Was this before or after I saw you, Douglas?" Beverly inquired. I could almost see her nose quiver like a hound on the trail.

"After," Uncle Doug said. "Probably around midnight."

Beverly nodded. But before she could start asking me any questions, I set the baskets of muffins on the two nearest tables and retreated. Grandma Kay followed me back to the kitchen a few moments later. She looked delighted with the way my big dramatic entrance as another character had worked.

The back door swung open and Mark walked in.

Big drops of rain glistened in his hair and slid off his jacket.

"There you are," Grandma Kay exclaimed.

"Yeah, I'm back to let those creepy friends of yours ask me the same hundred questions they did last night." Mark spoke lightly, but there was an edge to his voice.

"You should have seen him, Jen," Grandma Kay said. "It was masterful. With every question, he looked more and more like a pressure cooker about to explode. And then, when Beverly asked him how he felt to see you holding hands with another man, he stood up and stomped out. Even I wondered just a teensy bit if we'd see him again this weekend. Bravo, Mark," Grandma Kay finished. "I don't know how I'm ever going to pay the two of you back."

"I'll think of something," Mark said.

"Of course you will. That's why you're my favorite grandson."

"I'm your only grandson."

They grinned at each other.

"I can only stay twenty minutes," Mark warned.

"Who in their right mind would go biking today?" Grandma Kay raised her eyes to the ceiling, thinking. "Maybe if I call—"

"Don't you dare talk to my boss again," Mark interrupted. "Even if I do get off, I'm definitely not coming back here until after four. That was the plan, remember?"

"How's Aunt Lynn?" I asked quickly, since Grandma Kay looked like she was ready to argue.

Mark's face softened. "Much better. She and Dad

are planning on coming over after dinner to see the awards handed out."

"Excellent. Maybe they can help me sort through the solutions and pick out the best and the worst ones," Grandma Kay said. "Well, Mark, if you can only stay twenty minutes, you'd better get out to the sunroom. Your inquisitors await."

When I brought out another basket of muffins, I saw that Mark had sat at Beverly's table. He looked slightly bored as he responded to her question about how long we'd been engaged. But the rest of the people at breakfast were listening eagerly.

"And how long have you known Bri?" Beverly asked.

It was lucky that I wasn't pouring coffee into someone's cup because I would have spilled it. Bri? She wasn't part of the mystery. Had she stopped by for some reason last night and gotten roped into the plot?

"I can't remember not knowing Bri," Mark answered with a half smile.

"Ah," Beverly said. "The way she was perching on the arm of your chair last night made me wonder whether you were ever...close."

"Once. A long time ago," Mark said. He turned to Bri's mom. "Do you remember when it was?"

Mrs. Harris tilted her head as if doing a calculation. "Six years? Or was it seven?"

"That's about right," Mark said. "Bri ended it. We were both headed off to different schools. It was for the best."

I knew he meant different middle schools in real life, but his answer reminded me so much of Kent's excuse to break up that I didn't want to hear any more. But somehow, I couldn't leave. Instead, I stood there and twisted the pearl ring on my finger like it was an old, bad habit.

"It looks like Bri has had a change of heart," Beverly said.

"Too late for that." Mark lowered his voice. "I'm engaged. Remember?"

"Have you seen your fiancée since dinner last night?" Beverly asked.

Mark opened his mouth and then closed it. We had seen each other, but not in the context of the mystery. "No," he finally said. "But she probably needed to get off by herself. It doesn't surprise me that dinner with all of you would have that effect. She'll be back soon, I'm sure."

"Of course she will be, dear," Grandma Kay interrupted. "Helga, can you bring in more coffee, please?"

"Yes, ma'am," I said, and hurried back to the kitchen. Time to get back to work. I kept busy for the next few minutes carrying in baskets of muffins, plates of cinnamon rolls, and bowls of fruit.

No one other than Mark seemed ready to leave the tables when they finished eating. I couldn't blame them. Despite the dark clouds and steady rain, the breakfast room was bright and inviting. The green of the garden was almost tropical. The flowers looked like splashes of color in an impressionist painting.

After cleaning around the chattering group as best I could, I finally gave up and went to peel potatoes for the soup. As I sliced and chopped, people wandered into the kitchen, alone and in pairs, to interview my Helga persona on her movements of the night before.

When Uncle Doug's turn came, his private interrogation was on an entirely different topic.

"You didn't talk to Aunt Kay about things this morning, did you?" he asked.

I shook my head.

"I thought not. She looked too..."

"Relaxed? Normal?" I heard my voice rising. My fingers tightened around the handle of the paring knife in frustration.

"Hey, take it easy," Uncle Doug said in a calming voice. "We'll hash everything out tomorrow. It's easier for me, I'm sure, since I can distract myself with that other little puzzle. Hey, since you know what happened, maybe you could give me a few hints."

"Ha!" I said.

"Well, it was worth a try." Stuffing his hands into the pockets of his Dockers, Uncle Doug left the room.

The final cleanup after breakfast ran into the setup for lunch. To get everyone to leave the dining room, Grandma Kay finally had to announce that she was lighting a fire in the library. After I finished with the tables, I went into the kitchen and started arranging the platters of cheese and sliced meats. Grandma Kay dashed in and out periodically to check on the soup and my progress.

I was thinking about going upstairs during my break to read a few entries from my mother's journals when the door to the basement swung open. Beverly stepped into the kitchen. She must have slipped down the stairs when I wasn't looking. Her pleased smile reminded me of the Grinch.

"Helga," she said, "please go find the lady of the house. Something terrible has happened."

CHAPTER 16

Word spread quickly through the house that Beverly had found the body. Despite all the things I'd been going through in real life, I couldn't help but wonder about how the mystery turned out. So I joined the crowd in the sunroom to find out how I'd died. Mr. Boyd and I hadn't really gotten into that part of the mystery.

As the one who discovered the body, it was Beverly's job to read through the initial report aloud. A blow to the back of the head and a bruised cheek were the only obvious injuries. The head wound had been the cause of death. Blood was found on the edge of one of the crates. Further testing would reveal whether it belonged to the victim. No evidence had been found outside indicating that an attempt had been made to bury the body. Everyone agreed that anyone trying to dig a grave in the hard Missouri clay would have needed a pickax.

After Beverly finished, Grandma Kay herded the whole mystery group down to the basement to take a look at the crime scene. I returned to the kitchen to set up the lunch buffet.

"Beverly's timing was great," Grandma Kay told me as she finished arranging the trays twenty minutes later. "It provided a bit of excitement for the morning. Now that the time of death is confirmed, everyone will be checking alibis and motives even more closely over lunch. By about two, people will be ready for a break. They like to play games in the library, so we'll set up some card tables in there."

I kept busy during the meal, bringing out new trays and refilling the pitchers of ice tea. Once everyone finished, I cleared and set the table yet again, this time with Grandma Kay's best china and her wrought-iron candelabra.

At a little past two, I draped the washcloth over the drying rack and surveyed the kitchen. The counters and floor were finally cleared and clean. Dinner preparations wouldn't begin for at least another hour. If I went to find Grandma Kay to ask if there were any other things she wanted done, I knew that I would be trapped into conversation or some game. Quietly, I opened the door to the back stairway and began climbing.

When I reached the third floor, the hall was empty. I ducked into the linen closet to pull the wooden box from its place before heading to my room. As I inserted my key in the lock, the rasp of metal against metal seemed to echo down the corridor. I looked over my shoulder, half-expecting someone to appear. But Dorothy didn't pop her head out of a door with a request for my mother's address, Barbara didn't call up the stairs in search of a cribbage partner, and Beverly didn't suddenly show up for a private interview in her quest for the Marple.

I stepped inside and bolted the door behind me. I knew instantly that someone had been in my room: the pillows were more perfectly aligned and the door to the wardrobe was closed. I was sure I'd left it open on Friday afternoon as I'd dashed around looking for my keys before the drive into St. Louis. With a surge of relief, I remembered that Grandma Kay had gone through my things to find my pajamas, books, toothbrush, and uniform. But could she have been looking for anything else? I shook my head, trying to rid myself of all these ridiculous suspicions. I'd be glad when this mystery weekend was over.

I rearranged the pillows and flopped onto the bed, but I didn't open the box. Why was I hesitating? For the entire day, all I'd wanted was ten minutes alone with its contents, and now I was afraid to look inside. What would I find?

Start with the letters, I told myself. *There shouldn't be anything new there.* So I pulled out the letters and the baby book and compared the handwriting. For the first few paragraphs, I studied the loops on the Ps, the crossing of Ts, the bumps on the Ms and Ns. But within moments, I gave up the analysis and started to read. The words were so familiar that it was like revisiting a favorite book.

This time I noticed that the letters told me nothing about my mother's life—or at least nothing that had occurred in the time since she'd left Dad. One letter had arrived in the spring of fourth grade when Leah and I weren't speaking to each other. My mother had written about the trouble she'd had with her best friend Dorothy when they'd been rooming together at college during their freshman year. A letter about boys dated back to seventh grade when all the guys in middle school were swarming around Leah. I'd felt so reassured when my mother wrote me that hardly any of her male classmates had paid much attention to her until high school.

The way my mother always seemed to know what was going on in my life had made me feel like there was some kind of bond between us. And the obvious explanation—that she might have been receiving reports about me from someone we both knew—had actually been reassuring. It could have meant that, despite everything, she still cared about me.

My cell phone rang. I checked the screen, saw Kent's number, and turned off the sound. I didn't want to talk to him. I didn't want to talk to anyone. But seeing the time displayed on the phone made me realize that if I didn't start in on the journals now, I might not get a chance until tonight.

After rereading the entry about bears not being able to open doors, I turned the page.

May 2

Men are such babies. But I suppose I can't blame Roger for not wanting to see his cardiologist. From what I've heard, those stress tests aren't pleasant. And he insisted that the lab techs were vampires. "There's no way," he said, "that they need all that blood." But Kay told him that he was going to keep the appointment she made for him next Tuesday, no matter what. She said she doesn't plan to lose two husbands in four years. I backed her up completely.

The next page was blank; so were the ones that followed. The entry about Grandpa Roger was the last one she'd made before she left. Or was it the last one she'd made before she *died*? The entries didn't sound like the words of an anguished woman who was planning to abandon her family—who was planning to abandon *me*. I didn't want to think about that, so I reached for one of the earlier journals.

In it, I found more stories about me, like how I'd thought that squishing my peas and hiding them under my plate would be a tricky way to avoid eating my vegetables. Even though I was looking for it, I didn't find any reference to the first time that she'd left Dad. Or many mentions of him at all. There were a few times, however, when she wrote about going out to visit Grandma Kay at the Schoenhaus without him. That didn't seem like such a big deal.

As I read the stories about her coworkers, I could see why the characters of the mystery weekend had given Dorothy flashbacks. All of the backstabbing that went on at the accounting firm made work sound like a never-ending series of dramas. Maybe, I decided eventually, one of those strangers had had a reason to murder my mother after all. Then I turned another page.

September 20

I could kill Steve. I am still angry. Unbelievably angry. I even snapped at Jerry a few hours ago, even though the poor guy hadn't done anything.

Kay invited me out to the Schoenhaus while Jerry was finishing up his latest paper. When he's working, he can forget about eating and sleeping, even that he has a family. Kay wanted me to help her with some questions about estimated taxes and one of her portfolios. Doug usually handles all her money matters, but she didn't want to bother him—plus, she hates appearing like a complete financial idiot in front of him. "After all, I used to change his diapers!" she told me.

This morning, Jen and I took a walk through the vineyards. We were close to Steve's house when I heard Mark screaming. I swung Jen onto my hip, ran up to the house, and pounded on the door. No one answered. A second later, I was inside and dashing up the stairs. Mark stood in his crib, shaking the bars and howling. I set Jen down and picked Mark up. Naturally, Jen immediately started hanging on my leg and screaming. Mark wrapped his arms around my neck in a stranglehold and then proceeded to wipe his eyes and nose on my shirt. His diaper had a distinctly squishy feeling, so our first stop was the changing table.

It was a bit tricky, but I managed to pick up both Jen and Mark at the same time. I walked to the other end of the hall and pushed the door open with my foot. Steve lay sprawled across his bed, fully clothed and snoring loudly.

Just then I thought I heard someone in the hall, so I quickly closed the journal and slipped it under a pillow. After listening for several seconds, I was satisfied that no one was there. I pulled the journal out and found the entry again.

I almost swore, but Jen has a habit of repeating such words at the most inappropriate times, so I refrained.

I settled Mark in his booster seat. He downed the sippy cup of milk that I got him in ten seconds and then held it out to me for more. Instead, I handed him a plastic bowl of dry Cheerios. Then I sat Jen down in one of the chairs and gave her a few Os to chase around her plate. She can't stand it when Mark has something that she doesn't.

After the kids finished eating, I switched on Sesame Street. *Mark and Jen were both entranced. I ran upstairs and threw open the door to Steve's room. I couldn't hold in my anger any longer.*

"My head," was all he could say in between groans.

"What time does Mark usually wake up?" I demanded.

Steve looked at me as if he wasn't quite sure how I'd gotten there. "Seven."

"It's almost eleven."

Steve swung himself into a sitting position. I handed him the bucket that I'd brought for just such an emergency, and then turned my head while he vomited.

Steve just sat there with his head buried in his hands.

"This is neglect, Steve, criminal neglect."

"Is Mark okay?"

"Yes. But you're lucky he didn't try climbing out of his crib. He could have tumbled down the stairs, and you wouldn't have heard a thing. How often does this happen?"

Steve didn't say a word.

"I'll bet it happens more than you'd care to admit to me or yourself. A little one takes a lot of care. If this happens again, I'll go to Claudia and her lawyer and offer to testify on her behalf at a custody hearing. I'll do whatever it takes because Mark's health and safety come first."

My voice was trembling by the time I finished. Steve looked up at me, he had tears in his eyes. "What do I have to do?" he whispered.

"Pull yourself together," I said. "And get yourself some help. I'm not a doctor, Steve."

"My son means the world to me, "Steve said. "I'll do anything you say." He stared at me with those big, hungover basset-hound eyes. I shook my finger at him.

"I can't do this for you."

"I know."

I hope I wasn't making a mistake.

I flipped ahead to the next entry that had a reference to Steve.

October 1

Kay called me yesterday. She was absolutely delighted. Steve has been doing much better...

I paged through the rest of the journal, but didn't find any other mention of Steve or Mark until Christmas. Apparently, Lynn Spence had been invited over for Christmas dinner, and my mother sounded pretty pleased. Lynn, she wrote, would be much better for Steve than Mark's mother had ever been.

The journals and the letters all sounded and looked like they could have been written by the same person. If my mother hadn't written these letters to me herself, then who had known her well enough to write them?

I settled myself against my pillow and wondered what had really happened on that day my mother hadn't picked me up from day care. Had Grandma Kay violently objected to her daughter-in-law's plan to divorce her son? Had Uncle Steve decided to silence my mother after she'd caught him putting Mark in danger again? Or what if Dad...?

I sent my uncapped pen sailing across the room. It struck the wall, fell to the floor, and skittered across the polished wood. The telephone on the desk rang. I picked up even though I didn't want to. Grandma Kay might need me for something.

I cleared my throat. "Hello?"

"There you are," Grandma Kay said. "I'm afraid it's time to gear up for dinner. I've offered you to Ally Harris as a scullery maid. She likes doing the chopping herself, so you'll just be needed to help her find things, stir sauces, and clean up."

"All right," I said. "I'll be there in a second."

"What's wrong? You sound sniffly. Are you coming down with a cold or something?"

"No," I said.

"Don't forget about your outfit from Maddie. You may as well put it on now. You'll need to start trotting in and out of the library and parlor with appetizers."

"Do I have to wear it right now? What if I spill something on it?"

"Wear a big apron over it, silly. That should work just fine unless you spill a whole pitcher of something on yourself."

Now that sounded like a plan for ditching the uniform, but Grandma Kay would be suspicious if something like that occurred now.

As I pulled the shirt on over my head and tugged it

down over my hips, it felt even tighter than it had on Wednesday morning. I could almost see the outline of the extra cinnamon roll I'd eaten for breakfast. Instead of putting on my high heels, I dug a pair of black flats out of the closet.

Bri's mom set me to grating Parmesan cheese while she chopped. Her knife flashed up and down on the cutting board in a demonstration of skill that I'd only seen on television. I watched her in fascinated horror, afraid that she'd lose part of a finger.

"Your grandmother has let me make the Saturday night meal for the mystery weekend for the last four years," Mrs. Harris said. "I love to cook, but I hate all the cleaning that usually comes with giving a dinner party. So this is perfect. Besides, most of the clues to the mystery are planted Friday night anyway...unless there's a second murder, of course."

A second murder? Somehow I didn't think that was what Grandma Kay had in mind this time.

As we worked, Mrs. Harris went on to tell me stories of past weekends. Some I'd heard, but others were new to me. Like the time Mr. Boyd had gotten so caught up in the drama that he'd tackled a suspect. On one weekend, Beverly had cornered and ruthlessly interrogated a pair of innocent tourists when they'd dropped by in search of a room.

Then Bri's mom asked me whether I'd started in on college applications yet.

"Um, no," I said.

"It's never too early," she said, waving her knife at me. "In fact, you'd be smart to start getting some essay outlines together now."

Mrs. Harris chopped, pounded, and chattered while I followed her around and cleaned up after her. Clearly, the best way to fill out college applications was one of her favorite topics, but there was one that she liked even more: her daughter. Apparently Bri had stopped by last night and Grandma Kay had invited her to join them. She was now officially a part of the mystery weekend.

Just before five, Mrs. Harris sent me out to the library with a stack of small paper plates and a tray of hot stuffed mushroom caps and cheese puffs. I shouldn't have been surprised to find Bri at a table in the library playing cribbage with Mark and Mr. Boyd. She looked up from her cards when I walked into the room and laughed out loud when she caught sight of me in my costume. She leaned toward Mark and touched his shoulder, obviously pointing me out. Mark hid his mouth with his cards, but I recognized the same amused smile that I'd seen on Wednesday morning. Then Bri said something else in a low voice. Mr. Boyd and Mark both laughed. I decided to take the food to the other table first.

It looked like Mark and Bri were really cozy now. *It's the best thing,* I told myself. If I saw them together enough times, I would be completely cured of my ridiculous crush. When I reached their table, I kept my eyes on the tray as I held it out to them.

Every time I bent over, I could feel the back hemline of my short skirt creeping up my thighs. I was on my third trip around the library, this time with glasses of sparkling wine, when the phone at the front desk rang.

"Mark, could you get that for me, please?" Grandma Kay asked from her spot at the bridge table. "Helga is busy, and I'm right in the middle of a hand. I can be there in a minute."

Silently, Mark got to his feet and made his way out of the room. "Schoenhaus Bed-and-Breakfast," he said. He listened for a moment before saying, "Yes, she is. May I ask who's calling?... Oh. Hold on a sec."

When Mark returned to the library, he gave me a smug uncousinly grin. "Helga, it's for you."

"Who is it?" I asked.

Mark shrugged. "Guess."

Grandma Kay laid her cards down on the table. "You don't mean it's Kent?" she asked.

Mark let out an exaggerated sigh. "Helga was supposed to guess. Not you."

"Kent?" Beverly asked from her spot at the same table. "Isn't that Jen's other young man?"

I set the tray down on the nearest flat surface and rushed from the room, hoping that Kent hadn't overheard this conversation.

"Hello," I said.

"Hi," Kent responded. "How did the mystery go last night?"

"Really well," I replied.

"Do you still have an audience?"

"Yes. Actually, I do."

Kent chuckled. "I had a feeling you might. Sorry to bother you, but I couldn't reach your cell. We're trying to get a group together to go to Six Flags next Friday. I was wondering if you'd like to be my roller-coaster buddy."

"That...um...sounds fun," I said slowly. "But weekends are the busiest times out here, and—"

"Of course you can go!" Grandma Kay's voice carried clearly from the library. "Don't give it a second thought."

"As you may or may not have heard," I said dryly, "my boss said yes."

"Well, it sounds like you can't really talk now. I'll call you later this week, and we'll make plans. Okay?"

"That sounds great," I said.

"Talk to you then."

"Okay, bye," I said, and hung up the phone.

"What were you thinking?" Grandma Kay demanded as I came back into the room. "I'm not going to let a few unmade beds stand in the way of true love."

"I can cover for you, Jen," Bri said. "You know I owe you."

Mark just sat there. I couldn't read the look on his face.

I escaped to the kitchen. Mrs. Harris had left a couple of dirty cookie sheets in the enormous stainless steel sink. I attacked them with a scouring pad.

Just before dinner, Grandma Kay came in to give me my final instructions. "Serve from the left. Clear from the right. Keep the wine flowing. Don't ask. Just pour. People will leave their glasses more than half full when they've had enough. Fortunately no one's driving anywhere tonight."

CHAPTER 17

Is everyone finished?" Mrs. Harris asked anxiously as I returned to the kitchen with a stack of salad plates

"Almost. Beverly keeps picking up her fork every time I come near her," I replied.

"Hmmph," Mrs. Harris said. "She's just stalling, like she does every year. It may not be proper etiquette, but we can't hold up everyone else's meal because of her. Start serving on the opposite end of the table."

I did my best not to smile. Considering the care that had gone into all the dinner preparations, I could understand why Bri's mom was annoyed. Each potato-and sage-encrusted chicken breast was adorned with sun-dried yellow tomato butter and flanked by flat yellow strips of Parmesan polenta, steamed green beans, and sliced carrots.

As I served from the left, I listened to the group cutting apart Mark's means, motives, and opportunity.

"He couldn't have killed Jen," someone insisted. "I could tell by the way he looked at her that he was in love with her. He could never have done anything to harm her."

From the other end of the table, Mark inhaled, choked, and coughed.

Barbara thumped him on the back. "Dinner is always like this on Saturday night. Please don't take it personally."

When I carried the last plate into the dining room, Mrs. Harris followed me. She was greeted by loud applause. The meal she'd prepared had been a huge hit with the diners.

I returned to the kitchen and settled myself on a stool to eat at the counter. Mrs. Harris had made up a plate for me, too. I ate slowly, savoring each delicious bite. Then I started washing the first round of dishes.

Mrs. Harris briefly returned to the kitchen and topped each slice of chocolate almond cheesecake with a spoonful of freshly whipped cream. I slid my piece into the fridge and promised myself I would eat it as soon as I escaped from Maddie's dress.

Half an hour later, I finished collecting everything but the wineglasses, coffee cups, and saucers. As I moved past Grandma Kay, she reached out and touched my forearm. "Don't go yet," she whispered. "I want you here for this."

Grandma Kay tapped her fork against the rim of her coffee cup. Everyone looked up expectantly.

"Our revels now are ended, and it is time to expose the guilty party. But before you all go write down your best explanations for the murder, there are several people that I want to thank. Let me begin with Ally

Harris and her extremely successful efforts in the kitchen this evening."

Enthusiastic clapping and a few calls of "*Brava!*" echoed through the room.

"Next, please help me thank Barbara and Beverly for selecting the perfect vintage to go with dinner. Beverly donated the wine, but Barbara assures me that she gave her a very good deal."

Applause and laughter mingled. Grandma Kay smiled with obvious pleasure before continuing: "I must also thank the executive board of Ally, Steve, Lynn, and Barbara. They helped with mailings and all the small details that accompany an undertaking such as this. It was too bad that Steve and Lynn couldn't enjoy the fruits of their labor. But Lynn assured me that they will be here for the presentation of the awards."

Grandma Kay gestured toward the buffet, where two small bronze statuettes stood amid a pile of tiny wrapped packages. The Marple was a bronze bust of an elderly woman who wore a lively and inquisitive expression. The Christie was a nine-inch figure of Agatha Christie as a young woman. I had found out that afternoon from Mrs. Harris that Beverly had commissioned the traveling trophies from Aunt Lynn five years ago.

"We all thought it was so generous at the time," Mrs. Harris had told me in the kitchen. "But now it seems she just wanted something classy for her living room mantel."

"And that leads me to my last point," Grandma Kay said. "I'd like to thank my grandchildren, Mark and

Jen, for stepping up at the last minute to portray a most interesting young couple. I think everyone will agree that they did an admirable job. A very special thanks also goes to Jen for slaving all week on the last-minute preparations."

More applause.

"Now, before I send you away, I'd like to remind you of a few things. The Marple will go to the person who provides the most details to substantiate his or her case. But don't forget: incorrect statements will count against you. Take a form from Barbara on your way out. You have thirty minutes to put down your thoughts on paper. May the most insightful and crafty sleuth win!"

The room cleared in less than two minutes. After watching all the guests linger over the past three meals, I wouldn't have thought it possible.

Grandma Kay and Barbara joined me in the kitchen. They took on the task of washing the delicate china by hand as they quietly tried to analyze who suspected whom.

"And best of all, no one has even said a word about Jim Boyd," Grandma Kay hissed in triumph as she rinsed a dessert plate and set it on the rack to dry.

"Better not gloat, Kay. You haven't won the Christie yet," Barbara said. "Some cagey person may not have wanted to bring any attention to their suspect. But maybe. Just maybe." She glanced at the clock. "Let's go set up for the judging in the sunroom. People will start coming down soon."

In less time than I could have imagined, the kitchen counters began to clear. Cleanup was smooth since so much of it had been done during dinner and dessert. I turned off the sprayer and looked up as the back door opened.

Uncle Steve held the door for a pale Aunt Lynn. She walked directly to the nearest stool and sat down. She leaned her elbows on her knees and bowed her head.

Uncle Steve shook his head. "I knew we should have come in the car. You're exhausted."

"I'm fine. It wasn't that far. Hello, Jen."

"Hi, Aunt Lynn. I'm glad you're feeling better." I walked over and leaned against the counter next to her.

"She shouldn't be here at all," Uncle Steve complained. "She spent the entire day in bed."

"I was saving my energy for tonight," Aunt Lynn insisted in a weak but determined voice. "I haven't thrown up at all since this morning."

"That's so reassuring," Uncle Steve muttered.

"And I'm pretty sure I'm not contagious—" She stopped speaking with a sudden intake of breath. Her hand went to her throat.

"What is it? What's wrong?" Uncle Steve asked, moving quickly to her side.

"That's your mother's ring, isn't it, Jen? I never saw her without it."

"Really?" Uncle Steve said, squinting at it. "I never noticed."

Was he lying? What had happened between my mom and Steve after she wrote that journal entry? Had he murdered my mother and sent the ring? I didn't think so. He looked as out of it as ever.

"Ha. You hardly notice anything unless it's growing from one of your vines," Aunt Lynn said. "How did you get it, Jen?"

"It came yesterday in the mail addressed to Grandma Kay. There was a note with it."

"From Ellen?" Aunt Lynn asked.

I nodded, afraid to go into more detail. The poor woman already looked ready to fall off her chair.

"Then everything's all right, isn't it?" Aunt Lynn declared. "Thank heaven. I hated the thought that something might have happened to her."

Uncle Steve coughed. "Do you know if they're ready to start the initial judging, Jen?"

"Grandma Kay and Barbara are in the sunroom now," I said.

"Good. Ready, Lynn?" Uncle Steve offered her his arm and they left the kitchen together.

I trailed after them a few minutes later, hoping to find out which suspect Dorothy had picked. Even more importantly, I didn't want Grandma Kay to pitch those explanation essays once the judging was over. I'd spent enough time digging through the trash already this weekend. I started clearing the last few things off the tables.

"I don't believe it." Uncle Steve looked up from the paper he was reading. "Beverly isn't even close. She has this conspiracy deal going, a lot of nonsense about disappearing papers with things wound in about Kent, Bri, Mark, and Helga. You don't think we could give Beverly the "Completely Clueless" award, do you? She's really slipped this year."

"It sounds like there's hope. Has anyone even

picked the right suspect yet?" Aunt Lynn asked, looking up from her own pile of papers.

"Not yet," Grandma Kay said as she flipped through her stack.

"How did Dorothy do?" I asked. "Maybe she had beginner's luck."

"No," Barbara said. "She thought one of the junior partners was embezzling. Trust an accountant to go with the money angle. But wait a second." Barbara waved one of the sheets of paper. "Mark got the right suspect."

"Mark? You let him play?" Uncle Steve asked.

"I insisted on it," Barbara replied. "And why not? Everyone knew who the victim would be."

"It was probably just a wild guess," Uncle Steve grumbled.

Barbara grinned. "You're just jealous because *you* have gotten the Completely Clueless award every other year. No. It's all there. Mark got the motive. And he noticed that Jim slipped downstairs to look at the fresco while everyone cleared the table. And this line he wrote isn't really proof, but it's classic: 'I knew it had to be Jim because he was being so nice to me.'"

The iron candelabra that I'd been carrying slipped out of my fingers and dropped to the floor. Barbara's words echoed in my brain even after the clanging of metal against tile stopped. *He was being so nice to me...*

Instead of wondering all week who knew my mother well enough to write those letters, maybe I should have been asking a different question: "Who knew *me* well enough?"

CHAPTER 18

Everything had come together instantly in my mind. It was like a watching a scene from a film shown backward, the kind of scene when the shards of broken pottery leap off the floor to form a seamless vase. What did people kill for? *Love. Money. The guilt of hidden secrets.*

Grandma Kay, Barbara, Uncle Steve, and Aunt Lynn had swung around to stare me. "It...it slipped out of my fingers," I said. "I'm sorry."

"It's all right, Jen," Grandma Kay said. "Is it still in one piece?"

I dropped to one knee. My hands shook as I reached out to pick up the candelabra. "Two of the candles are broken, but otherwise..."

"Really, it's fine, Jen," Grandma Kay said. "You don't have to be so upset about a little accident."

I smiled weakly at her and retreated to the kitchen to pace back and forth. My suspicions only grew as I tried to poke holes in my frightening theory. I struggled to take a deep breath, but the maid's costume was like a steel cage around my ribs.

I still needed to find some evidence before it disappeared, too. I stopped myself at the basement door with the realization that I shouldn't imitate the dimmer heroines of film and fiction and go down there alone.

I left the kitchen to look for Mark. When I reached the library, I spotted Dorothy, Uncle Doug, Beverly, and Mr. Boyd at a table. Beverly was shuffling a deck of cards with the speed and skill of a Las Vegas dealer. A few other weekend guests, whose names I'd never learned, sat on the sofa in front of the fireplace. I finally spotted Mark in the corner.

I went over and leaned down to whisper in his ear. "I need to you to help me get something out of the basement."

"Can it wait or minute or two?" he asked. "Bri made me promise to wait for her here. She said she'd be right back. But if it's important—"

"No, that's okay. You can come down after she gets back," I said, trying not to feel annoyed. At least he'd know where I'd be.

"I'll be there in a bit," Mark said.

I was pretty sure I'd be back upstairs before he came to join me. It shouldn't take me very long to find what I was looking for. And everyone else was busy.

I left the basement door ajar behind me, like a thief entering an airtight safe with no handle on the inside. Leaving a trail of open doors and burning lights behind me, I returned to the unfinished half of the basement—and the room where an imaginary womanizing lawyer had disposed of an equally fictitious promising first-time novelist.

I closed my eyes against the brightness of the naked bulb that hung down from the ceiling. It left a ring of orange against the darkness of my eyelids. Then I looked in the corner at the hand-lettered sign propped on the bottom layer of the step pyramid. "Congratulations!" it proclaimed. "You have found the body."

I studied the stack of boxes. Grandma Kay had recorded the contents and the year of each crate in her nearly illegible scribble. I saw that the box I'd hoped to find was right there on the bottom. But that made sense. These papers would be over fourteen years old.

I was shifting the boxes off the top layer when I heard footsteps. "Mark??" I called.

"No," Uncle Doug said as he came around the corner. "He's still upstairs."

"Hey, what's up?" I asked.

"I saw the look on your face when you left the library and wondered if you were coming down with Lynn's stomach bug. So I went to the kitchen, found the door to the basement open, and followed the lights."

"Yeah, I...uh...lost some beads off my dress last night and thought they might have fallen off down here. Mark was going to come help me look. But you know, now that you mention it, I actually don't feel so great."

Uncle Doug nodded. "You don't look too good."

Suddenly, I really did feel sick. I clapped one hand to my mouth and extended the other to warn him away from me. I swallowed hard. A tiny voice in the corner of my mind observed that it was a very good thing I hadn't eaten the chocolate almond cheesecake.

The spasm passed. Uncle Doug circled around to my right, no doubt intending to put a supportive arm around my shoulder while remaining out of the line of fire.

I took an involuntary step back.

"Jen, what's wrong?" Uncle Doug asked.

"What did Ellen say to you that day?" I asked in a harsh, grating voice that I hardly recognized as my own. "Don't tell me. I can guess. *This is criminal, Doug. Criminal. And to think that Kay asked me to look at things that she didn't understand because she doesn't like looking like a financial idiot in front of you.*"

Uncle Doug stared at me as if I were possessed. Maybe I was. "What are you talking about?" he asked.

"What did my mom find?" I asked. "Did you steal money from Grandpa David's estate? The documents are right here in this pile of boxes, aren't they?"

"Jen, this is ludicrous. I would never steal anything from Aunt Kay."

"So what happened? You just borrowed some and hadn't gotten around to giving it back yet? My mom believed in second chances. I know she did." I paused for a second to pull some air into my lungs. "But you killed her anyway."

"I did no such thing!"

"You asked me when Dad was leaving for his conference so you could slip into our house and steal the letters. You sent the package with the ring, knowing that it would arrive on Friday. Then you got rid of the envelope it came in so no one could check the postmark. You calculated exactly how Grandma Kay would react, and you were even there to pick up the pieces. The whole time we were digging through the trash, you knew we weren't going to find anything."

"No."

"What's another lie to you? Every letter to me that you forged in my mother's handwriting was a lie. All the years I've known you have been lies."

Uncle Doug suddenly seemed to crumple. "Jen, I swear I didn't...kill your mother. But...I did see her die."

I took another step back. So it was true. I hadn't really believed it until I heard Uncle Doug say it.

My mother was *dead*.

"You're right," he rushed on. "There was an irregularity. A buying opportunity that I couldn't pass up. I had the money to cover it, but I couldn't get at the funds right away. Ellen must have noticed something. She set up the meeting at the Schoenhaus. I was in hell for days, thinking that Aunt Kay knew. But it was just the two of us, me and Ellen. I showed your mother how I'd returned every penny with interest. She said she'd noticed that. If she hadn't seen that I had paid the money back, she would have revealed everything. I swore I'd never do it again.

"She agreed not to expose me, and I followed her out to the porch. She was standing at the top of the steps. She was still angry and...and she turned around too quickly...and then she fell. I couldn't reach her in time. Her head made this awful thud when she hit the concrete walk..."

Uncle Doug's face was ashen. He took two deep breaths before going on. "I ran down the steps and fell to my knees beside her. I called her name. She opened her eyes, but seemed to stare right past me. She told me to watch out for you. Then she didn't say another word."

"But...," I croaked. I cleared my throat and tried again. "But the porch steps aren't that high."

"A fall from any height can kill a person. My heart nearly stopped last night when you stood in the very same spot and almost did the exact same thing. But I didn't fail you the way I failed her."

True, but something didn't seem right. "If it was an accident, why didn't you call the police?"

Doug threw up his hands. "I wanted to, Jen, but I couldn't. I knew they'd say I had means, motive, and opportunity. Isn't that what the crew upstairs has been chattering about all weekend?" he asked. "I didn't know what Ellen had told your father or Dorothy. Someone would have looked into Aunt Kay's finances. And the only witness to the fact that I didn't lay a finger on your mother was lying there dead. I figured that no one would believe my story."

"But couldn't you have left her there so someone else could...find her?"

"That would have been even worse. If I had done that, the police would have searched the house and they would have found the documents. Someone undoubtedly would have said they'd noticed a red convertible in the area around the exact time that your mother died. I can see now that you're right. I should have called the police. But instead, I panicked. And I felt so awful about what the whole thing had done to you. The guilt was just tearing me to pieces. That's why I sent that first present on the first Christmas after she was...gone."

"After she was *dead*," I corrected.

Uncle Doug rubbed his forehead. "I thought I could keep her alive for you. I wanted you to know what a wonderful person she was. No one else would talk about her, especially your father. And any child psychologist would probably tell me I did exactly the wrong thing. But you were such a stubborn, difficult child. You responded to those letters. Jerry could say the same things until he was hoarse and you wouldn't pay him one bit of attention."

"I've always wondered...how she could know...all those things about me when she wasn't around," I said, taking a breath after every few words. "Now I know." My heart beat unevenly in my chest. Not another panic attack. Not now. I had to stay calm.

Uncle Doug looked at me, his pale brown eyes filled with anguish. His hands twitched at his sides as he stepped closer. "You believe me, don't you, Jen? No one else has to find out about this. Aunt Kay has given up. I've done everything I could to make it up to you and Jerry. And there's no body."

"Yes...there...is," I said as an overwhelming rage practically choked me. "Or there *was*. Where did you put her?"

"Can't you let your mother rest in peace, Jen? I swear that she's in a beautiful place." Uncle Doug's eyes flicked to the chalk outline of the body on the floor.

I knew he couldn't have hidden her somewhere in the basement. Every one of the mystery guests had agreed that it would take a pickax to dig in the hard Missouri clay. I stared at the wilting white petals of the rose. No one had moved it when they came down to check out the crime scene.

Then I knew. "The roses," I breathed. "She told you about Grandpa Roger planting the roses right by the steps. All that loose dirt. That's where she is, isn't it?"

"Jen!" Uncle Doug's expression darkened. "Can't you let it go? I swear to you—" He stopped speaking as the machine-gun clatter of footsteps sounded on the stairs.

"Mark!" I shrieked.

Uncle Doug took a step back as though I'd slapped him. "I guess I have your answer," he said.

My uncousin appeared in the doorway. Panting, he looked from me to Doug. "What's going on?"

"Ask Jen," Uncle Doug said. He slipped past Mark into the hall.

Mark walked across the room toward me. "Okay, I'm here. What's wrong?"

I tried to breathe so I could answer, but the air rattled in my throat. The room started to go dark.

CHAPTER 19

"She's not supposed to be dead, too, is she?" I heard a confused voice ask.

"She's dead," I answered.

"I think she said something," another voice said.

"No," I said irritably. "She really *is* dead."

"There. She said something again."

Gradually I realized that, while I was talking about my mom, the voices were talking about *me*. I must have fainted or something. I took a deep, shuddering breath and opened my eyes.

My head was cradled against someone's shoulder.

There was another burst of questions, but I heard the voice in my ear the most clearly.

"Jen, what's going on?" Mark demanded. "What happened?"

I pushed against Mark's chest and rolled out of his lap. I knelt on the cool, clay floor, not daring to stand, and stared up at the circle of faces around me. Some of them looked confused; others, concerned. A few seemed to be enjoying the latest chapter in what they thought was just another part of the mystery.

I smoothed my tiny skirt over my thighs, trying to stall long enough to control the rage rising in me again. I managed to take one deep breath before lashing out. "This has all been a lot of fun, hasn't it?" I shouted. "Someone died. Fabulous! Whoever could have done it? And Kay and Ally are such wonderful cooks and the rose garden is so lovely this year and Beverly will win anyway because she always does. But not this year."

Now everyone's face wore the same look of stunned confusion.

"Jen?" Grandma Kay asked, stepping forward. "Whatever—?"

"Well, someone else is dead, all right," I went on in a ragged voice. "And since your stupid game is over, why don't you all just leave?"

Embarrassed guests stampeded for the door. Mark, Grandma Kay, Uncle Steve, Aunt Lynn, Barbara, and Dorothy stayed.

My grandmother came closer, holding out her hands to me. She, at least, could recognize the difference between drama and reality.

"Jen, talk to us."

"She's...she's been here all this time," I said, my voice breaking. "Easter. Christmas. Birthdays..."

"Who?" Uncle Steve asked, frowning. "Who's been here?"

"Ellen," Grandma Kay breathed.

"She didn't want to leave me and Dad," I said, my voice breaking. "She didn't know it would turn out the way it did. Neither did he."

"Your father?" Grandma Kay asked.

"No, Uncle Doug. She caught him taking money from Grandpa David's estate. Then there was an accident..." I paused, unable to utter the words aloud. "She's in the roses," I whispered. "*Under* the roses."

My attempt at an explanation sounded demented even to me, so I tried again. "Grandpa Roger had been working in the front flower beds. The ground was already loose..."

Grandma Kay covered her face with her hands. "No. Oh, no."

Uncle Steve put both arms around her. Then he glared at Dorothy as if to ask why she hadn't left with everyone else.

"Ellen was my best friend," Dorothy said quietly. "I can't believe she's gone. I had no idea..." Her eyes welled with tears.

"Are you absolutely sure about this, Jen?" Barbara asked.

I couldn't answer. I wasn't sure of anything anymore.

"What are we going to do?" Grandma Kay's voice shook.

"Well, first we need to let the guests know what's going on," Barbara said. "Or tell them something, anyway."

"Yes," Grandma Kay said. "As long as Jen is comfortable with that."

"All those people," I said, groaning. "I need to tell them I'm sorry."

"I'll deliver your apologies, Jen," Barbara said. Her eyes had teared up, but her tone was steady. "They have to stay tonight. It's getting dark; the roads are wet. And everyone had plenty to drink tonight."

"Tell them I didn't mean it."

"Yes, you did," Barbara said. "But who can blame you?" She looked at Mark. "Could you help Jen? She looks as if she might collapse again. "

Mark's arms went around me. I hadn't realized I was shaking until then. He held me firmly and pulled my head onto his shoulder. "I am so sorry, Jen."

"It all seems so unreal. How could I...I mean, how could he—"

"Hey, shhh. It'll be okay," Mark said in my ear.

"Sometimes I hated my mother for not being there," I said, choking down a sob. "And she couldn't help it."

"Jen," Grandma Kay broke in, "we need to get you out of that tight dress. No wonder you fainted. I'm not going to forgive myself for any of this for a long, long time. If I'd had any idea—"

"You would have gone full speed ahead," Mark said.

"Mark," his father protested.

"It's all right, Stephen," my grandmother said. "I deserved that. But Mark, I had no idea that this weekend would turn out like this. And I never expected that Douglas would...that he had..." She shook her head. "Douglas was like a son to me." Her voice was hard and cold as she used the past tense.

CHAPTER 20

An hour later, I found myself sitting in an upholstered leather chair, a bit uncertain as to how I'd gotten there. My mind seemed focused on odd details: the flowered pattern around the rim of my teacup, the pearl ring on my finger, the plaid of the blanket Grandma Kay had draped around me.

I knew a few things. Uncle Doug was gone. His red Miata wasn't in the parking lot. And everyone was waiting for the police.

"I am *not* leaving," I heard Aunt Lynn tell Uncle Steve. "I feel fine. I have to make sure Jen is all right."

"Sure. You'll be a big help to Jen if you collapse," Uncle Steve muttered.

I glanced up to see Aunt Lynn clutching the armrests of her chair as if she expected her husband to pick her up and carry her off. When she saw me looking at her, she relaxed her fingers. "Jen, honey," she said. "Why didn't you tell any of us? You shouldn't have had to go through that alone."

I sensed rather than saw Mark stiffen.

"I don't know," I said.

"Don't know?" Grandma Kay whirled around, nearly upsetting the lamp next to the sofa. "What other things have you been hiding from us?"

"I found my mom's journals."

"Journals?" Grandma Kay looked stunned. "Where? When?"

"In Dad's closet. After the envelopes turned up missing."

"Missing?" Grandma Kay repeated. "Jennifer Emily Schmidt! Why didn't you tell me any of this? And why didn't Jerry—" Grandma Kay stopped and put her hands to her cheeks. "Oh, my poor boy. How am I ever going to tell him about Ellen?"

"I'll do it," I said. "Can I use your phone?" I asked Mark.

"But, Jen," Grandma Kay said. "Shouldn't we wait until your father's here? Or at least until we know more?"

"Now," I said.

Mark silently handed me his cell phone. I flipped it open.

"But we're not sure—," Grandma Kay began.

"I'm sure."

I punched in the number. *Pick up*, I thought. *Pick up*. Dad might not answer if he didn't recognize the number.

"Hello?"

"Daddy?" My voice squeaked. I hadn't called him that for years.

"Jen, honey, what's wrong?"

"It's about Mom. We think we know what happened to her."

"You do? Where is she?"

I took a deep breath and tried to keep my voice from shaking. "Under the rosebushes at the Schoenhaus. I'm...I'm sorry, Dad. She's been here all this time."

I heard a long, shaky sigh, and then nothing for several moments.

"Dad, are you still there? Dad?"

"I'm here," he said. "What...I mean how—? No. Never mind explaining right now. I'm going to get the first flight out that I can. Are you with Mark right now? I see you're on his cell phone."

"Yes."

"Good."

"Everyone else is here, too," I said. *Except Uncle Doug,* I added to myself.

"All right, then. I'll call you back as soon as I have my flight info. Hang tough, honey."

"Okay," I said. "Bye." I shut the phone and handed it to Mark.

At the sound of footsteps in the entryway, we all turned toward the door. A few seconds later, Barbara ushered in a pair of police officers. Drops of rain speckled their shoulders.

"Good evening, ma'am," one of them said to Grandma Kay as he stepped forward. He held his hat in both hands. "I'm Officer Jordan. This is Officer Williamson."

"My goodness, that was fast," Grandma Kay said.

"Ma'am?" Officer Jordan said.

"You're here about the body, aren't you?" asked Grandma Kay.

The policeman's frown deepened. "You already heard?"

My stomach dropped. I sensed there was going to be more bad news. So, it seemed, did Grandma Kay. She backed into an armchair and sat down. "Heard what?"

"I'm afraid there's been an accident. You're an emergency contact for Douglas Schmidt?"

"He's my nephew."

"I'm sorry, ma'am. He lost control of his car, just east of the Vinchgau Winery on Highway 94. We believe he was killed instantly."

"Oh, no," Grandma Kay gasped. "Oh, no."

I didn't faint again. I only wished I could. Uncle Doug was dead, and it was all my fault.

CHAPTER 21

I pulled my mom's journal closer to my face and squinted in an attempt to make out a scribbled word, but it was impossible. The twilight had deepened into near darkness. I rested the book on my chest, closed my eyes, and felt the hammock swing gently back and forth. I saw a few lights turn on at the Schoenhaus. It was hard to believe that almost two weeks had passed since the mystery weekend.

The police had taken all the other journals from my room at the Schoenhaus for possible evidence, but they'd allowed me to keep this older one from Mom's college days. When I told Dad about finding them in his closet, he didn't yell at me. Instead, he sat down and started telling me story after story about my mom, from how they'd met, to the night I was born, to things that happened just before she disappeared. I listened in amazement as the words poured out of his mouth, almost hypnotized by the flashes of the gold wedding ring on his left hand as his gestures sketched pictures in the air. He hadn't worn that ring for as long as I could remember.

In a strange way, Dad had gotten his wife back. I had gotten my mom back. But we'd both lost Uncle Doug in the process. He would have been lost to us even if he hadn't died in the accident. I kept thinking about the agony in Uncle Doug's face during his confession. Sometimes it didn't feel right to blame him, even though he'd buried my mother's body under the rose garden, where she'd lain undiscovered for almost fourteen years.

So now would Uncle Doug be the person we never talked about?

There hadn't been any skid marks near the site of the crash on Highway 94. Had Uncle Doug's red Miata hydroplaned off the wet roadway? Or had he kept control of it all the way into the tree that killed him? The accident had happened on a dangerous stretch of road within a few hundred yards of where that silver Mercedes had passed me at the beginning of the summer. I played the events of that night over and over in my head, trying to imagine a way I could have changed things. I finally gave up.

I would never know exactly what happened to Uncle Doug. I only knew that it was my fault, one way or another. It had been my words and my fear of him that had sent him off into the rainy night.

My dad and I had sat beside Uncle Doug's girlfriend in the front row at his funeral. She didn't want to believe what had happened that night. I didn't either, so that was one more thing we had in common. Grandma Kay had refused to attend.

The clanging buzz of the cicadas rose above the hum of the other insects. Like an insistent alarm clock, it encouraged me to start moving. The mosquitoes would start biting soon. I closed the book, swung my legs out of the hammock, and stood up.

When I was halfway to the Schoenhaus, I saw someone moving across the garden toward me.

Mark had come to both funerals—Uncle Doug's and my mom's. He, Kent, Leah, and even Bri had all hovered around me as though they were afraid I'd drop and shatter at any moment.

I waved at Mark and then sat down on a bench to wait for him. He was there beside me a moment later.

"I didn't expect you back so soon," he said.

I shrugged. "Grandma Kay will be reopening the Schoenhaus to new guests this weekend. She's not worried about reporters sneaking around anymore. We're old news."

Mark looked down at the book in my hand and asked, "How many times have you read through that?"

"A few."

Mark gave me a sad little half smile. "I wonder if it's a good idea for you to stay out here. Bri could probably take over until Maddie's arm gets better."

"So you want to get rid of me?" I asked in a joking tone. But not so very deep down, I meant it.

"Of course not," Mark said. "Lynn thinks you should be getting out and going places and thinking about other things."

"I'm meeting Dorothy in Augusta for lunch on Saturday."

"I'm pretty sure that's not what she meant. Don't get me wrong," Mark said quickly. "I like Dorothy. I like all of the people in that crazy group. They really stepped in to help: cooking, cleaning, picking up your dad up at the airport. You name it, they did it."

"True."

"You were pretty out of it for a while," Mark said.

"Yeah, I was. But I'm better now. And I am getting out a bit. I went to the zoo with Kent yesterday."

Mark leaned back against the bench. "Oh, really? And?"

"We talked."

"And?"

"And nothing. We're friends."

Mark frowned. "I saw the way he was hanging all over you at Uncle Doug's funeral."

I shook my head. "It's over. It just wouldn't work out between him and me, for all the reasons that we broke up in the first place. And..."

"And what?"

"Well, there's this other guy," I admitted.

"Oh yeah? Who? With everything that's been going on, you haven't had time to meet anybody—unless it's one of the guys from basketball."

I shook my head. If he hadn't figured it out by now, I wasn't going to tell him.

Mark's eyes widened. "Wait a minute. You mean...?"

"I'm not exactly thrilled about it, either," I said. "Don't worry. I'm sure I'll get over it soon. And if you can forget I ever said anything, I'd be very grateful."

"Jen." Mark's voice was gentle. But I had become accustomed to that. Now he had another reason to feel sorry for his uncousin.

"What?"

"What if I don't want to forget it?" Mark asked slowly.

I stared at him.

"You really don't get it, do you?" he said. "Everyone else that weekend seemed to figure it out."

"You were acting."

"I must be a rotten actor, then. I was trying to play things really low key. That's why I didn't get up right away and head down to the basement with you that night. If I had, maybe your Uncle Doug would still be here."

I slid down the bench until our thighs touched. "It wasn't your fault."

"I don't know about that."

"I do," I said firmly, even though it had taken me until that very second to realize that I shouldn't be blaming myself either. "Uncle Doug should've never gotten behind the wheel. Not after everything that happened." I sighed and shook my head.

An indescribably light hand caressed my cheek. Then Mark's lips touched mine for a long moment. I pulled back and murmured, "This could be a really bad idea."

"Yeah," Mark said, pushing my hair back from my face. "I'm surprised Grandma Kay hasn't shown up already. Should we go inside and break the news?"

"No," I said. "Not yet."

The End

KRISTIN WOLDEN NITZ learned the subtle art of planting clues from reading—and often rereading—hundreds of mysteries. The historical buildings, sloping vineyards, and winding roads around Augusta, Missouri, gave her both the initial idea and the eerie atmosphere for SUSPECT.

Kristin, who is also the author of DEFENDING IRENE and SAVING THE GRIFFIN, grew up playing basketball in Duluth, Minnesota, She now watches track meets with her husband and three children in southwest Michigan.

www.kwnitz.com